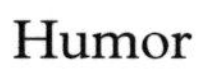
Humor

illustrated by the same author

HOLLOWAY
Robert Macfarlane, Dan Richards
& Stanley Donwood

HUMOR

Stanley Donwood

FABER & FABER

First published in 2014
by Faber & Faber Ltd
Bloomsbury House
74–77 Great Russell Street
London WC1B 3DA

Typeset by Faber & Faber Ltd
Printed and bound by Martins the Printers Ltd, Berwick upon Tweed

A CIP record for this book
is available from the British Library

ISBN 978-0-571-31243-6

2 4 6 8 10 9 7 5 3 1

To

M + I + K

Contents

Introduction ix

SANGUINE 1
PHLEGM 65
CHOLER 115
MELANCHOLY 147

Introduction

It happened every year. The first year it was not too bad; just a scream that died in my throat upon waking. The details of the dream were already cloudy in my mind; all I knew for certain was that it had been very, very bad. This was when I still had nightmares. I had a lot of nightmares, but this one was particularly unpleasant.

Everyone has bad dreams; some more than others, some dreams worse than usual. What bothered me was that each year I had the same nightmare, but each time the dream contained the next part, the next . . . chapter. The events of this dream refreshed my memory of the previous one, and there was no doubt about it: it was a continuation. I became a little worried and I sought out books about dreams to salve my thoughts. I hadn't paid much attention to books about dreams, but now I found out that there were many. A number of them dealt with the interpretation of dreams, but I wasn't very convinced by them. I didn't think that my dreams needed interpretation; they just needed stopping.

I read Freud on dreams and Jung on dreams; I read R. D. Laing and I read a very odd and disturbing book called *Lucid Dreams* by Celia Green.* Lucid dreams are

* Published by the Institute of Psychophysical Research, Oxford, 1968.

dreams in which you know you are dreaming. This alarmed me, as it indicated a fraying of the fabric between wakefulness and dreaming, and the dreams I was having were starting to suggest to me that any sort of fraying of this kind would be extremely dangerous. There were demons in my dreams and I had absolutely no desire to let them out.

I was perhaps a little crazy. I thought that the nightmares were real, that what happened in them was as important as, or equal to, what happened to me during the day. The fear of the next chapter of one dream in particular – the one that was, I realised, due any time now – bothered me a great deal.

And naturally it came. It was indescribably terrifying, a horrific, ghastly, full-colour epic featuring baskets full of severed heads, interminable periods of supermarket shopping, an electrifyingly fearsome man who continued to live and speak after I had smashed his brains out in a fireplace, and extremely beautiful rural scenery.

I woke up, wrenched out of the nightmare as if dropped from a helicopter, pouring with cold sweat, wild-eyed and panicking. I knew now that the 'man' I had killed (but not killed) was a demon, or a devil, and that he/it was a particular demon; he was my demon. I felt hopelessly awful; this had, indeed, been the next part of the particular dream I had feared the most, and it was definitely getting 'worse'.

I wasn't even sure if it had been a year since the previous chapter . . . Surely it hadn't been? The details of the dream, now, showed no signs of clouding, no amelioration by the daylight. The dream was at least as real as the attic room I slept in, probably more real. It had certainly been convincing. As far as I knew all earthly laws of physics had been adhered to within the dream; perspective worked normally, birds sang in trees, rabbits scurried away at my approach. Even the details were right: the top bar of a gate had been worn by use, patinated with human touch; species of tree were clearly identifiable; the baskets full of severed heads were real baskets, woven from willow, smeared with blood. Dreams were not supposed to contain supermarkets, certainly not supermarkets with special offers and litter blowing in the breeze outside. The only thing that had not been real was that fucking demon.

I was absolutely terrified. The border where waking life met dreaming life seemed to be in the process of fracturing, and if that happened there was no predicting what might happen next. I couldn't sleep. That was completely out of the question, utterly unthinkable, if I were going to stay normal and not get any crazier than I already felt. Staying awake, however, brought with it several consequences.

One of these consequences, with horrible irony, was that my ability to determine whether I was asleep or awake became compromised. It got harder to know which was which, because fighting sleep is exhausting, and an exhausted body craves sleep intensely, no matter what the brain attached to that body may wish for. The body and mind become disassociated, and I became clumsy, forgetful and vague. This was not working.

Sleep returned to my life and with it came a blizzard of nightmares, but these were merely awful tremors. I lived in fear of 'the big one'. What I was most concerned about was the fact that 'the big one' carried harbingers of my death: not my death in life, but my death in the nightmare. That demon wanted me with a coldly implacable desire, and when he got me I would die in that nightmare and that's where I would stay, in some unspeakably nasty eternity, everything repeating itself, round and round, unbearably. I knew that there were only a finite number of chapters in that nightmare, and with each chapter the end came irrevocably closer. The end of the dream was the end of me.

I began to take steps to protect myself. My housemates found me chalking the letters LIVED on the soot in our fireplace, as I was convinced that the hearth was a possible entry point for the demon. Somewhere I had read that this was an effective strategy, the theory being that if the demon sees the word DEVIL written backwards he will return to where he came from, tricked into thinking that he's in a mirror-world.

I also began to write my nightmares down. This started as a way to keep track of them, to make absolutely sure of the sequential nightmare, to record and identify any possible channels of resistance. Themes began to emerge: supermarkets, the early hours of the morning (just before sunrise), medieval and Tudor architecture, aliens, demons (obviously), transmogrification, hauntings, enormous evergreen hedges and landscapes that were eerily reminiscent of golf courses, with trees spaced at equal intervals and closely-mown grass.

I edited the written versions ruthlessly, cutting out swathes of text. There was no sense in trying to contextualise these night-time journeys, no point in attempting to fit them with a beginning or an end. As far as I could tell these frightening excursions were all middle. I wrote in the first person, naturally, and in the present tense.

I decided to dilute my dreams by sending these written versions to a disparate group that I had been corresponding with for several years, in a kind of one-way mail-art. If enough people read the dreams they would dissipate, their power dispersed into the ether like some sort of noxious vapour. I made small booklets and placed them in envelopes, posting them with a sense of slight relief. This was a cathartic offloading of internalised menace that I hoped would help calm the night. I called these booklets *Small Thoughts*.

At this time I had been working with Radiohead on the record that was to become *OK Computer*, in a large mansion house not too far from where I lived. I came across a book about the art of Jean-Michel Basquiat, and I ordered the book of symbols** that he had used as a reference while making such paintings as *Untitled* (*Pecho/Oreja*) and *Untitled* (*Per Capita*).

The symbols were a revelation. As well as many that found their partially erased way into the artwork for *OK Computer*, there was exactly the mark I was looking for. It was a hex, a magic symbol that would bring bad luck and misfortune to demons. Hexes are normally very bad;

** *Symbol Sourcebook: An Authoritative Guide to International Graphic Symbols*, by Henry Dreyfuss, published by McGraw-Hill (1967). This is the book in which I first came across the medical notation sign meaning 'NO DATA', which I consequently used as the title for two separate exhibitions.

certainly not the sort of thing you'd like to find scratched onto your front door. This one, however, was extremely useful. I started using it immediately, chalking it on walls (and also, of course, on the soot of our fireplace) and reproducing it in various pieces of artwork, some of them used in the *OK Computer* artwork, others on t-shirts and posters. The more places where the symbol was inscribed the better; I was very pleased to engineer the pasting of Barcelona's streets with enormous posters bearing not only the symbol – large, black on white – but also, unmistakeably, the words AGAINST DEMONS.

Meanwhile I was writing more and more of the nightmares down, pinning them to the page like speaking moths. The internet was another canvas on which to pour these expulsions, and at the same time as building the first version of radiohead.com I started compiling slowlydownward.com. This eventually led to the first publication of the written dreams in book form, as the first edition of *Slowly Downward* was published a few years later, using texts the publisher Ambrose Blimfield took directly from the website.

Over the course of a few years the dreams were read by many people, either from the booklets, from a circular tin of dreams, from a bag of dreams, from the website, from the Radiohead artwork I inserted them into, or from the book. The 'Against Demons' symbol had travelled all over the world, thanks to Radiohead's punishing tour schedules, and I had seen photographs of it turned into a tattoo.

It is impossible for actions not to have a consequence, and so it was that my nightmares ceased utterly. In one dream I learned the name of my tormentor, which helped a lot, but overall I believe it was the concerted attack that stopped it all. The chapters never advanced any further, and eventually even the mild nightmares passed.

However I do slightly regret their disappearance, as now, of course, I have nothing to write about. Although I remember enough to be extremely careful what I wish for.

Stanley Donwood, 2014

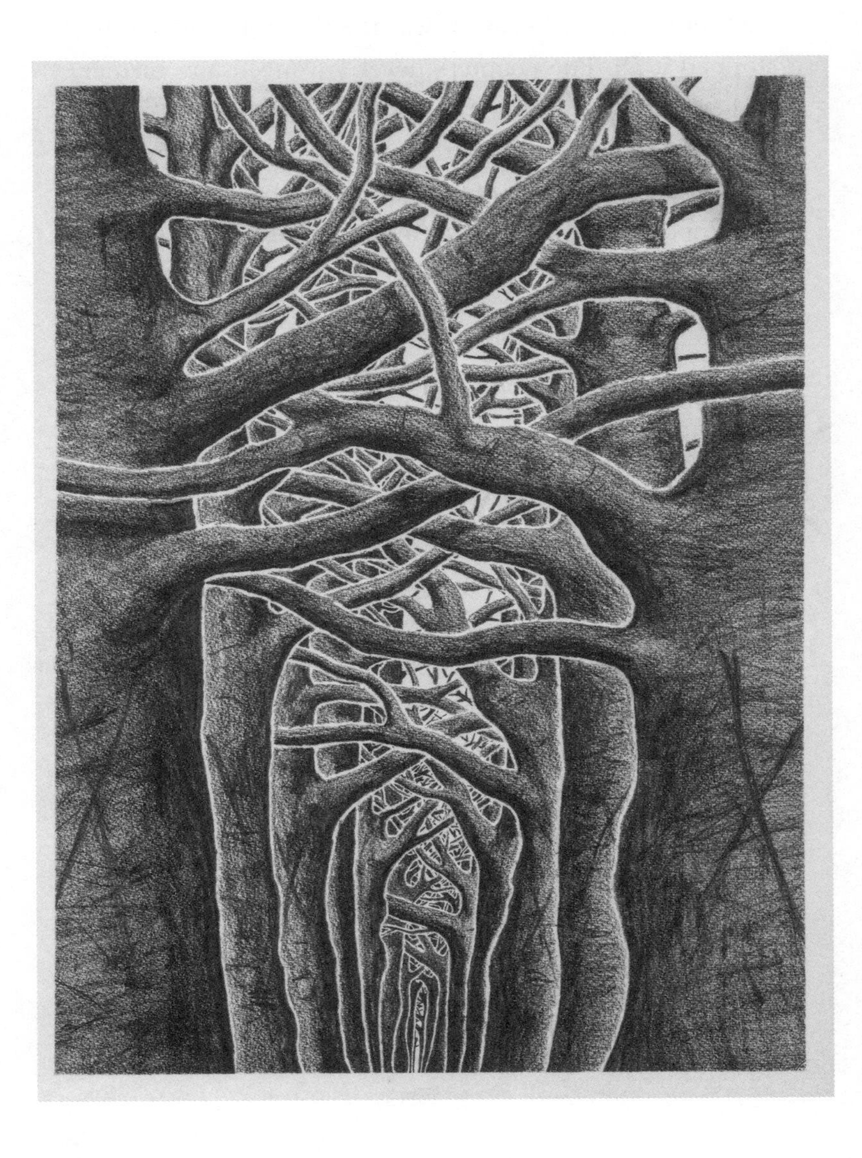

SANGUINE

Happiness: A Guide

No one is happy and if they say they are they're fucking lying. And I should know; I've tried it. I've collected all the ingredients of happiness and rubbed the resulting mixture all over myself.

Not many people have done it. It's extremely difficult to get any of the ingredients in the first place, let alone all of them. Mixing them properly is also very challenging; a lot of people get it totally wrong by concentrating on one ingredient at the expense of another; an easy mistake to make. What you have to do is lie in wait for each, be patient while they congregate (which doesn't often happen) and then saunter over, introduce yourself, and invite them back to your place. Metaphorically speaking, of course.

But it doesn't end there. It's not simply a matter of assembly; you've got to add various sorts of seasoning if the whole thing isn't going to end up like some nauseating religious marzipan. What you want is an easily absorbed lotion that won't bring you out in a rash or make you smell.

Beware of commercial preparations, expensive luxuries, evangelical tautologies, meretricious platitudes and printed hyperbole. Anything that promises fast results or pain-free acquisition should be avoided. Real happiness is, as I've said, incredibly hard to attain, requiring years of struggle, hurt, anguish, self-doubt, paranoia, and lengthy periods of agonising melancholy. Anyone who tells you different is either fooling you or themselves.

Personally speaking, I have overcome these many obstacles. And you can too, if you're willing to work at it; but, to be brutally honest, it's not worth it.

Scent

I got into a fight in the perfume department of a large store. It wasn't my fault; I had been trying to choose a nice scent for my new girlfriend and there was a scuffle to my left. The perfume ladies backed away. I was filled, at the time, with a sense of invulnerability that came with having recently fallen in love, and I stepped forward to quell the incipient violence.

Naturally I was punched, knocked over and kicked in the face, but the broken bottles of perfume released such an incredible bouquet that I afterwards remembered the encounter with a degree of fondness.

My Week

SUNDAY

Turned on the telly. On BBC1 was *I'm So Lonely*. On ITV was *You'll Never Be Famous*. Thought of cranes, pylons, dams, volcanoes, locusts, lightning, helicopters, Hiroshima, show homes and ring roads.

MONDAY

Read that for men under thirty-four the biggest killer is car accidents. Second is suicides. Spent a while wondering what third was. Hit my head against the wall a few times.

TUESDAY

Something without a name has been eating at my thoughts for a while. Standing in the checkout queue at the supermarket I feel violent, or bored, or hopeless, or depressed, or pointless, or just sick inside. Need only to see a headline of someone else's newspaper to feel frightened, or frustrated, or alienated, or helpless, or doomed, or just suicidal. Waking up was a battle with my limbs; stodgy, unreliable, wayward, hurting.

WEDNESDAY

Woke up. Found I'd forgotten how to tie my shoelaces. Basic cognitive functions then failed with increasing rapidity until all I could do was sit in a chair staring at the wall.

Tried to phone for help but my arm wouldn't move. Eventually

THURSDAY

FRIDAY

SATURDAY

Sky Sports

One day I found out that my urine was acting like a powerful foaming agent. I thought that I could take advantage of my ability by hosting piss-scented foam parties in the pub toilets, but the landlord wasn't keen. He didn't think that people would be interested. In fact, he said that it was a disgusting idea. I said I'd rather go to a piss foam party than watch the fucking football, but he said that I'm in a very small minority and the big screen stays.

Fingers

It is only after I have been at my new flat for some months that I begin to receive mail other than bills and offers to enter prize draws.

One of my first personal envelopes contains a scrawled message from an old acquaintance with whom I was friendly many years ago. I am distressed to read that my friend is deeply unhappy, and I am disturbed further to read that if he receives no reply to the letter I hold in my hands he will feel compelled to chop off one of his fingers with a kitchen knife. Days pass, full of inconsequential incidents, until a small parcel arrives. The postmark indicates that it is from my friend. With trepidation I open it.

Underneath the brown wrapping paper is a little box that bears the return address of my friend. There is also a stamp on the box, but other than this the package proves to be empty. I open up the box, but the space within is likewise vacant. A sense of relief floods briefly through me, and my days once more assume a comfortable aspect.

One week later, another identical parcel arrives. It too is empty, and I insist to myself that I will write to my friend. Time drifts past, and eventually I have ten empty parcels. It is on a Friday that I realise what I have to do.

With what I feel is admirable forethought I use my left hand to chop three fingers from my right. With the remaining two, I hack off all the fingers of my left hand. In considerable pain I place the fingers in eight of the parcels. There is a lot of blood, and this makes the use of Sellotape difficult. With eight parcels wrapped, I hold the knife in my right thumb and forefinger. I look at the last two boxes. As always, it is my inability to complete any task that drives me to tears.

Dracula

It is summer, and I am persuaded to take a Continental holiday by two enthusiastic acquaintances. Being a creature of habit, I am accustomed to vacations in the seaside resorts near to my home, but the proposition is put in such a way that I find it hard to make excuses.

We depart, and travel by train to Romania, where, after a series of misadventures, we are all captured by Count Dracula, Prince of Darkness. We are taken in a foul-smelling horse-drawn carriage to his castle, which towers blasphemously above the forests, fingering the torn sky with its crumbling turrets. We are, naturally, rent with terror. It is clear that the Count intends to drink our blood, turning us into undead monsters of the night in the process.

We are imprisoned in once-luxurious apartments, overlooking Dracula's estate. It is evident that the twentieth century has not treated our host well. Ominously, he tells us in heavily accented English that he has been forced to open up large tracts of his estate as a theme park, with log flumes, bowling alleys, rollercoasters and burger bars, all of which are frequented by Western tourists who know nothing of the old ways.

Our sympathy is tempered by the sure knowledge that the Count intends to suck out our souls with his pointy teeth. We secretly devise a daring plan to flee. We encourage the Count to show us round the theme park, and, as we come to the bowling alley, hurl ourselves down the planks into the skittley darkness. We scramble through wires, pipes and other obstructions until we find ourselves in an area devoted to crazy golf, where we mingle with the tourists. It is with some relief that we exit through the turnstiles. It is easy from thence to find a hire car and complete our courageous escape.

Back home in Eastbourne, I wonder if we did the right thing. It infuriates me that Dracula may have needed my soul more than I do.

Head and Shoulders

When I moved to my new flat I was very happy but when I worked out that the whispering voices that I can hear when I put my head under the water in the bath belong to dead people I wasn't happy any longer, particularly because I realised that every time I put my head under the water when I had a bath the voices were slightly louder than the time before.

I tried not putting my head under the water when I had a bath but every fucking time curiosity got the better of me and I had to try it just for a second just to check and of course even half a second of that sort of thing would bother anyone.

I keep asking the landlord to put a shower in but he prevaricates and says things like what do you want a shower for that's a lovely old bath that's an antique that is look at it it's Victorian you'd pay top dollar for one of those at the reclamation yard.

It's all right for him. He hasn't got fucking dead people talking to him every time he washes his hair.

Nearly Got

One night I am alone in my house, compiling lists of friends from the past. It grows dark, and I begin to wish for company. The list sits before me on the table, reproaching me with intimations of missed opportunities and regretful abandonments.

There is a scratching at the window, and absently I open it, assuming that one of my cats is feeling lonely too. To my dismay, a small devil-creature, salivating with anticipation, leaps squatly into the room. I recognise it immediately as being of the type to possess the soul without hesitation.

Backing away from its gleaming eyes, I consider my options. With a flash of intelligence, I announce to the devil-creature that it is yesterday, and today I am dead. The creature looks quizzically at me. I insist that it has made an error – it is yesterday, and later this evening I kill myself with a large, sharp kitchen knife. I am dead. My soul has gone. The devil-creature is too late.

It looks puzzled, but I explain, with placatory hand movements, that this is really a simple matter. As I am already dead, there is no point in attempting to take my soul. Come back in a week, I tell the devil-creature. The landlord will have re-let the house, and there will be fresh prey. Huffing and puffing, the creature waddles back to the window, and lurches off into the night.

Congratulating myself on my quick thinking, I close the window. I sit down once more in front of my list, and it is with a heavy heart that I wander into the kitchen and begin rifling through the knife drawer.

Bond James Bond

The world is at terrible risk from hideous and malevolent Alien monsters and it is up to me to do something about it.

Luckily I stumble across an Alien podule which can take me up to the huge war satellite that is circling Earth. It is a squeeze, but I get into the podule and quickly comprehend the Alien dashboard and launch into space.

Within minutes I dock with the war satellite and effect my egress. The satellite is a maze of chrome corridors, and I creep along them in my silent, rubber-soled shoes.

I take my Beretta from inside my dinner jacket as I hear a faint cough in the distance. I pass along more corridors and through several chrome rooms the size of cathedrals until I near my quarry.

I peer around a doorway and am surprised to see a famous professor from Earth. Swiftly I attack him. When I kick him in the stomach, he collapses like a sack of heavy air.

I pull him to his feet and interrogate him. It seems that he has been creating Alien monsters with an evil Alien academic who wants to take over the planet Earth. At first he assumed the Alien was well intentioned, but the monsters they made were increasingly violent and deranged.

He introduces me to his first monster, who is very courteous, but I am told that all the subsequent monsters would tear my head off at the slightest provocation. I decide to let the professor go, for the time being, and, hefting my Beretta, I go in search of my nemesis.

New Job

After a tortured night I awake full of determination.

I review my position, and consider with circumspect gravity my inner strength. My new job demands much, and I eat my breakfast while wearing a serious and adult expression. I suck the hot coffee with a professionally pained mouth, and flip the pages of my broadsheet nonchalantly.

I swoop back up the stairs in my towelling dressing-gown, and fling open my wardrobe in a manner that I assume to be casual and easy. My suit hangs in front of me, full of nothing. It is up to me to fill it with myself.

I pull on the trousers, and carefully fold my penis behind the zip, fastening the button with what I hope is a manly grin. I tuck my shirt into the trousers, and spend some time with my understated tie.

My jacket feels slightly small under my arms, but it is nothing anyone would notice.

I wonder what my new workmates will be like, and fantasise briefly about the relationships I may possibly enjoy with other members of the organisation.

I glance once again at my digital watch, and decide that I am ready. I pull on my coat, check that I have my keys, and walk out of the front door, slamming it firmly behind me.

I stand outside, looking blankly ahead, realising I don't have a new job at all.

Loyalty Card

I am in the foyer of the supermarket, an empty wire trolley idling beneath my imperceptibly trembling fingers. The light is bright, and the smell is of nothing at all. My mind is blank. There is a route to be followed: straight ahead, turn right then right again, travelling aisle by aisle until (I am planning ahead) I end up in the wines, beers and spirits. My experience in these matters tells me that I will have run out of money by then, unless I am careful. I will have to be careful.

But, almost immediately, things start to go wrong. Here I am, transfixed by the twitching red muscles in the meat aisle. This isn't very good. I take a deep breath and move away. Nothing to see here. There is the rattle of teeth, of fingernails, bones, in the cardboard cereal packets, sloshings of lumpy fluids in jars and tins, and the muffled howls of the doomed. I jerk my head away from the cans of 'processed meats' and the hanks of hair in the salad bags.

In the frozen-food cabinets; plastic sacks of severed fingers, cling film stretched fetishistically over pale limbs bent double and tied with white string, blood pooling darkly in the polystyrene trays.

Death warrants – signed, but with the name left blank – among the Sunday papers.

I can't do it. I can't shop. Looking determinedly straight ahead, I remove a bottle (whiskey? vodka? I am unsure) and stand in line at the checkout. Do I have a loyalty card? I stare in fear at my interrogator.

'Yes,' I whimper. 'I mean, no.'

Airborne

One rainy day whilst out shopping for groceries, I am surrounded by a growing crowd who are under the impression that I can fly. It seems that a dreadful mistake has been made: the local paper has printed an article about a gentleman who really does have this enviable talent, but they have put my photograph above the article. I am unsure about how the newspaper came to have a picture of me, but that is the least of my worries, faced, as I am, with this heckling crowd of strangers. I protest, but the crowd will give no quarter until I show them my incredible powers.

At last, I give in to them, and stand, flapping my arms and jumping as high as I can into the damp air. This goes on for some time, and I become increasingly frightened that the now-disenchanted crowd will attack me, believing me to be a self-promoting charlatan. But in the end they straggle off, muttering. Thanking my lucky stars, I rush home, too upset to continue my shopping.

That evening, alone, I once again try to fly. It proves to be a futile exercise, but addictive. Night after night I stand on my roof, flapping my arms and making small jumps on the tiles. Try as I might, I never manage to get airborne.

Futile Gesture

I find myself in a responsible position within a reputable institution, and my evening arrival at home is welcomed by my beautiful wife. We share many interests, and spend pleasantly frequent hours discussing cultural matters. Our house is more than adequate for our needs, although we both ruefully agree that if we were ever to have children a relocation could be in order. But in the meantime we enjoy our life together.

One evening I am suddenly conscious of a noise from the kitchen. I ask my wife to pause the video, and pace uneasily towards the door that leads to it. I walk softly in my stockinged feet towards the door. I pick up an empty wine bottle and slowly turn the handle. I feel more animal than human, more ready to deal with an intruder than I ever have before. I burst open the door, the neck of my wine bottle in my clenched fist.

There is nobody in the kitchen. I give the back yard a cursory check, but the flat feeling I have tells me that nothing will be there.

Determined to make something of my foolishness, I pointlessly grate some Edam cheese. I almost continue the grating until my fingers are bleeding, but I decide that it would be a futile gesture. I return to the living room for the rest of the video, leaving the Edam to curl and atrophy in the kitchen.

Chip Shop

Despite my reservations, I am wandering the streets of the town in the company of several people with whom I have little in common. The evening has been dominated by seemingly random sallies into pubs populated almost exclusively by large men in vests, with whom I have absolutely nothing in common.

Every glance upwards reveals a sky that has been soaked the colour of lager. Every time I attempt to join in the obvious jollity of the occasion I am drowned out by the inadvertent yelping of my compatriots, and I resort to adopting a vacuous yet friendly expression whenever any enquiry is directed in my direction.

We stand in a huddle of indecision outside a brightly lit doorway, and earnest debate falls around my ears as I watch, with unbelieving nausea, a chef in the chip shop opposite shoo a flaming, but living, pigeon from the window of his establishment. The flying, sputtering lump of flame erupts from the window. My attention is distracted by an enquiry from my colleagues regarding money. I answer with rapidity, only to turn my gaze back to find the burning bird has disappeared from my view.

After an eternity of boredom we emerge from the club. The pigeon is lying in the gutter, curiously expanded, horribly burnt, utterly dead.

Haunted

While I am searching for an old diary in the attic, I find a large cardboard box full of ring-binders, which, in turn, are full of notes I once made concerning the construction of an emotional puncture kit.

The find seems providential: my love-life is in tatters. Constructed almost entirely of half-truths, fabricated intuitions and vaguely remembered urges, my private life is transparently in desperate want of repair. If ever I needed the emotional puncture kit, it is at this emotional juncture.

Unfortunately, I need to locate several parts to build the puncture kit, and despite many pleading telephone calls to various ironmongers, greengrocers, bookmakers, stationery shops and butchers, I am unable to assemble the kit.

I look out of the window, and notice that tumbleweed is blowing past the house. The sight adds to my increasing depression, and I hasten to the town to actively seek the parts I need.

A pawnbroker's catches my eye, and I step inside the musty shop. I explain my predicament to the papery man behind the grille, and he shows me a box that houses some small rodents. The pawnbroker tells me that the rodents may not replace my love-life, but they will love me if I love them. And if I fail to love them, they will punish me with their sharp teeth.

Not quite knowing why, I buy the rodents and hurry home. Once there, I tell them sweet things, and get them a saucer of milk.

Later, my husband returns. It seems that he has successfully sold my old diary to a major publisher. I am oddly unmoved, but then, I have my rodents.

Statue

I am commissioned by a wealthy opera singer to carve a marble sculpture of her torso. Without shame, she disrobes, and I make preparatory drawings, noting the lines of her voluptuous curves and the weight of her voluminous tresses.

An enormous block of marble is duly delivered to the velvety chamber where I am to carry out my trade. Confidently I take up my mallet and chisel, and begin to rough out the statue.

Days pass, then weeks, and after a period of many months I announce to my patron that the work is complete. She stares for some time at the fruit of my endeavours. Something is not right. I sense that she is displeased in some way. I shoo her from the chamber, order another block of marble, and begin again.

I am enshrouded in dust, I work through the night, until my fingers are raw and my breath comes in harsh rasps. Again, my employer is unaccountably dissatisfied.

I continue to order marble, and continue to carve statue after statue, while the years pass.

When, eventually, I create a marble likeness of the opera singer on her deathbed with my own wizened and arthritic fingers, she at last nods, smiles, and abandons herself to the relentless pull of eternal sleep.

I place my chisels carefully on the floor, and lie next to her, placing my dusty hand in her cooling fingers.

Seaside Town of Vampires

My holiday takes me to a resort for which I have distant but fond memories of innocent pleasures and fine bars. I wander the littered streets until I find my favourite cantina, now flyblown and murky. The proprietor fails to recognise me, and I order a coffee.

Sitting outside in the wan sunlight I am depressed by the changes that have taken place in this once-beautiful seaside town. Many shops are boarded up, the youth seem preoccupied with the dusty ground, and the cinema has been transformed into a seemingly unpopular bingo hall.

Worst of all are the diminutive vampires who bowl along the promenade biting the legs of passers-by. The only way to deal with these pointy-toothed parasites is to kick them viciously into the harbour. I entertain myself morosely in this way for about half an hour, sustaining only slight scratches from the fangs of these riviera nosferatu.

Things are not what they used to be around here. The thought reminds me uncomfortably of my ageing body, and my own desire to live vicariously the lives of others.

I realise that although I can understand the sad plight of the vampires, I cannot resist the urge to kick them, flailing, into the grey ocean.

I return to my room, and sit at the window. If there were an observer, I imagine that they might see the cloud-scattered evening sky reflected in my dark pupils.

Laboratory

I obtain a poorly paid job in a dusty laboratory. The afternoon sunlight falls into the room through yellowing venetian blinds, and I pass the time making tea and answering oblique questions desultorily during collapsed conversations.

As time passes in its tedious way I slowly become aware that the experiments taking place in the laboratory are at best sinister; and at worst evil. At least 80 per cent of the hypotheses are obviously invalid and intended to support revolting surmises.

I increasingly spend most of my time in the kitchen, staring at the limescale that bedecks the overflow of the sink. I fancy that I can see emergent civilisations in the crust that grows daily around the tap bases. The weeks fall through my fingers.

Eventually the experiments become too much for me to tolerate. Mice are being sacrificed to a nameless dark presence that hovers over the building, manifesting in the dust, colouring the minds of the scientists with whom I am forced to spend my futile daylight. Somehow the laboratory is filling my dreams with fear.

I soon recognise that it is the mouldering soul of the building itself that is engineering this mounting horror. Quietly, during my tea-making duties, I plan my escape.

I realise that if I mention my discontent to my co-workers all exits will be closed to me.

At last, with a daring flourish of courage, I attempt to effect my egress. It is with a dreadful terror that I realise the door is locked. I turn, and see the hollow eyes of the scientists upon me. There can be no escape.

Big Bird

Whilst on a walking holiday in remote regions, I chance upon a secluded valley, away from the popular walking routes. Some distance along the valley I come across a scene so breathtakingly beautiful that I drop to my knees in wonder. There is something about the serried ranks of deciduous and coniferous trees standing tall on the opposite bank of the river that sets my heart ablaze. The colours of the foliage are poetic, while the arrangement of species seems divinely inspired. Clouds swoop and whirl above the topmost branches, and the river sparkles through an uncertain reflection below.

Suddenly, the sky darkens, and along the river advances a flotilla of huge birds with menacing eyes. The size of the birds staggers me; one is as tall as a bus, and the others not much smaller. Their plumage is a shimmering blue, but their eyes are full of hate and looming disaster. With a horrible sinking feeling, I realise that the birds have noticed me. One of them clambers up the nearside bank, and waddles towards me.

I take to my heels, and scramble along the path. Gaining speed, I run at full tilt. Then I see people in front of me, running towards me. First one passes, then another, then another. They are wide-eyed with terror, and keep taking quick, fearful looks behind them. There must, I realise, be something unutterably horrible in front of me, but my fear of the big birds compels me to carry on.

More people run past me, all with the same frightened expression. They are running towards the birds, away from something unknown. I am running from the birds, towards something unknown. Not for the first time in my life, I curse my bad luck.

Machete

I work as a personal bodyguard and I am employed by a gentleman who fears for his life, threatened, as he is, by dark threats of sickening violence delivered by unknown persons over the telephone.

After some preliminary investigations, it becomes clear that the telephone calls are an invention produced by the imagination of my client. Nonetheless, his fear is real and I begin to wonder if, despite appearances, there may be some truth in his fears. My hunch proves right when, one night, my client's guttural screaming summons me to his bedroom. There, shifting from foot to foot and hyperventilating with feral excitement, is a foul creature from the underworld. The demon takes one look at me and seems to dismiss me as a minor player in this drama. He is waving a large machete at my client, relishing the fear this engenders. My client is blubbering at me to do something.

In fact, I had suspected that demons may have been at the bottom of this job, and have taken the precaution of acquiring a phoney machete of flimsy wooden manufacture. I tease the demon with childish taunts, and, as he rushes at me, I dextrously swap the machetes.

It is only very slightly later, when my client's head is sliced off, that I realise I have made an error. My career is finished.

Burning Pub

While drinking coffee in my usual bar I am joined by a group of friends. A couple of hours pass in a pleasant manner, and as evening darkens the sky I am persuaded to join them for a bibulous meander.

As the sun creases into a bank of simmering cumulus, consensus decrees that we visit a bar close to the meat-packing district. A relatively brief walk, and our destination is within sight. Pigeons scutter overhead, and I am reminded of my jacket which I must collect from the dry-cleaner's. The blackened city curves over our passage, and we halt for a group consultation of the *A to Z*.

I notice a flash of light in the corner of my vision, and turn swiftly. Across the road, within the plate-glass windows of a large and busy pub, sudden flames billow and swoop towards the ceiling. I stare, clamped to the pavement with disbelief. A surge of light blasts from the pub windows, which are now completely filled with incandescence. I stand open-mouthed, unable to communicate the horror that is coursing through me, merely ululating monosyllabically.

As suddenly as they flared, the flames disappear. Within the pub, the customers continue their evening. With gasping breaths, I attempt to explain what I have just seen to my friends.

It is a nuclear-holocaust theme pub, they explain. Nothing is real. I am unable to deal with this, and make my way home through the echoing streets with tearful eyes.

Rubbish Time Machine

Having at last completed work on my time machine, I am disappointed to find that it does not work beyond the parameters of my own life. I can travel back to my childhood years, observe myself behaving insufferably as a teenager, see myself as a tottering octogenarian; in effect I can visit any period of my relatively mundane life, but cannot travel to the past that I missed or the future I will never see. To compound this problem, I cannot actually touch, taste or smell anything during my already uninteresting travels.

No one in the past or future can see me. I attempt to speak with myself, warn myself about imminent dangers, shout 'don't marry her', and so on, but all that escapes the confines of my mouth are little puffs of carbon dioxide. The whole time-travel thing seems horribly reminiscent of my experience at parties.

Back in my laboratory, I extricate myself from the spidery apparatus of the time machine, and stare wearily from the bleary windows.

A Wet Night

I am invited to a party that is being hosted by some old friends. As usual, I get to the party early and stand awkwardly outside the gates to the house. It is dark but warm, and unknown creatures speak to one another in the night.

I step hesitantly into the overgrown garden, and notice a light on in the house. Although the party may not have started, I convince myself that my hosts need help with the preparations. I am a dab hand at samosas.

Easing my way through the conifers that bar my progress, I approach the lighted house. Intending to play a minor joke, I peer in through the window, and I am surprised to see two Aliens from Outer Space conversing in the drawing room. They appear to be engrossed in a clever discussion, and I withdraw quietly, not wanting to disturb them.

After loitering outside the front gate for some time, I make my way back home, now sure that the party is either not going to happen or that I have inadvertently entered another dimension.

About a week later, I come across one of my old friends in a café. He asks me why I wasn't at their party. I make my excuses and leave.

My brother calls me at home, and we discuss our respective social lives. My brother complains of a boredom with life, while I counterpoint with a distrust of parties in general and clever Aliens in particular.

Eventually, we agree to finish the conversation, but as I put the phone on the hook I am seized with terror. Quivering, I run a bath, aware that both my reactions and my emotions are ill placed.

Love Story

I am driving a fast car along the beautiful cliffs that line the road between London and Brighton. My mind is aflame with lust. To my left gleams the azure Mediterranean, while on my right the chalk cliffs flash in the sunlight.

I am increasingly worried as the car gathers speed, as it seems that my brakes have been sabotaged. Faster and faster, the cliffs flick past. I am forced to do some clever manoeuvring until I skilfully skid to a halt in Brighton, where my lover awaits, resplendent in a velvet-lined apartment overlooking the shingle beach.

We engage in inventive sexual games while hooligans roam the wet streets below us.

On Sundays Ring-Road Supermarket

I am queuing at my nearest out-of-town supermarket when an unpleasant scene begins to develop. Three shop assistants haul a muscular but dead young bullock out from behind the translucent flaps that guard the inner sanctum of the store, and lay it on the tiles in the tights, socks and toothcare aisle. Another assistant emerges with several large knives, and the four of them stand around the carcass as if awaiting silent instructions.

As one, they flash their knives and one of them makes a large cut in the hide of the bullock. Another slices deftly at the neck area, while the third and fourth make incisions around the jaw. The two assistants nearest the head lay their now-bloody knives on the clean tiles, and, with visible effort, insert their fingers into the gashes they have just made. They begin to pull at the thick, hairy skin of the bullock, tugging hard until the flesh begins to pinkly emerge. They pull and pull, and the hide slides back over the jaw. As the skin comes back, to my horror, the bullock's eyes begin to flicker.

At the moment the hide rips back over the eyes, they widen, and the bullock staggers to its feet. The assistants pull harder and harder, but the bullock charges away towards the delicatessen counter, its face flapping wildly around its flayed skull. I am close to fainting, although I cannot, as I have been queuing at the checkout for what seems like an age. At last, my items are scanned and I pay for them, my Visa card shaking in my hand.

Aztec Procession

I am sitting outside my favourite bar, drinking coffee and smoking quietly. In the distance, through the heat and softly settling dust of siesta-time, I hear a faint clattering and chanting. I turn towards the sound, straining my ears.

After several minutes have brought the noise closer, I realise that it is the music of a grand religious procession of some kind.

My suspicions are confirmed when a colourful scene bursts into the stillness of the square. In the centre of a mass of Aztecs are a royal couple, hoisted up on an elaborate double throne. The Aztecs are all expressionless, their eyes blank and dead as they chant and sing.

I glance nervously around, but I am the only person in the square. The bar appears long closed, and my coffee is cold. As the Aztecs turn to stare vacantly at me, I feel certain that I should be elsewhere.

I unfold from my chair and bolt along a narrow alleyway between tall buildings, the washing lines flapping high above my head as the baleful roar of the Aztecs echoes from the square. I run this way and that, my heart pounding and my face streaming with sweat. I am lost, and in a blindly unreasoning panic.

Acting with Certainty

I find myself alone in a frightening building at the dead of night. I am filled with an eerily familiar mixture of fear and rage. I reason that I could either curl up on the floor and whine pathetically or take responsibility for my inner anxieties and act with certainty.

I decide on the latter, and call out the name of my personal demon and psychic tormentor. I repeat this shout with increasing volume several times, until he appears, reeking of evil and smouldering foully. My fury overcomes a sudden feeling of spiders crawling in my duodenum, and I launch myself at the demon, screaming an assortment of obscenities, pummelling him viciously. As I punch, he seems to diminish in size. I continue to beat him, until there is nothing left of him except his Doctor Martens boots, which I fling from the window into the night with a callous laugh.

Subsequently, I am unable to sleep at nights, as I worry greatly that there may have been something of the demon still left in the toes of the boots. I attempt to find them, but the frightening house is not on any street in my town. Weary now from sleeplessness, I wait in my room for the demon to return, and regret deeply having behaved so decisively.

Trouble with Neighbours

The hazards of city life take their toll, and I move to a small seaside town built of wooden houses. Unfortunately I become involved in a dispute with my next-door neighbour. That matter escalates to the point where he feels the need to involve his hard-drinking friends.

One evening, drowning my sorrows at the tavern, I learn that my neighbour plans to burn down my house. The information distresses me considerably, and I decide to take evasive action. Returning to my house, I turn on all the taps, and with a hose I drench the walls and contents of the building. I sneak out of the flooded kitchen and hide in nearby sand dunes.

Sure enough, later that night my neighbour and a gang of angry drunks approach my house with flaming torches. In vain, they try to set fire to the soaking wooden structure, but it is simply too wet to catch light. Hidden in the dunes, I chuckle with delight at having outwitted my neighbour.

The next day, in the grocery store, I am pinned to the wall by the shopkeeper. He tells me he is good friends with my neighbour, and accuses me of underhand tricks. I tell him I don't know what he means, but he says no one but me would deliberately drench their own house with water simply to spoil his neighbour's fun. He tells me that kill-joys like me have no place in a real community.

At home I sit on the wet sofa, pondering the nature of my existence. Later I wander the house, turning off the taps, one by one.

Game

I am disturbed to discover that my colleagues have invented a new game which seems to involve attempting to kill me in every juvenile way that presents itself to them. They delight in surprising me with shoves into the paths of oncoming double-decker buses, constructing ridiculous rope-and-pulley devices with the aim of dropping heavy furniture on my head, placing tripwires at the tops of escalators, and other such inanities.

They persist for some weeks, during which I become increasingly adept at avoiding sudden death by blackly humorous means. I feel that my senses are sharpened day by day, that my sight is keener, my reflexes quicker.

Soon I can detect by the smell of linseed oil alone the presence of a cricket-bat-wielding acquaintance in the bathroom. Everything is enhanced. Colours are richer, noises are louder. I awaken to the pattern of life, the weight of deeds.

Eventually my heightened awareness evolves into a vividly focused paranoia. I can only retreat; I move surreptitiously to a small seaside resort on the east coast and wait, slowly, for a death of my own choosing.

A Quiet Afternoon

I am alone in a hot city. My favourite bar is closed for siesta, and I am aimlessly walking the dusty streets. Outside a shabby tailor's, I am accosted by a man in a dark suit. He acts in a conspiratorial manner, and invites me to follow him along the street.

After some time, we arrive at a small bar on the edge of the city. We take a seat each, and the man whispers to me that he is suffering from an unusual complaint, in that he is consistently late for everything. He explains that this is because somebody has stolen his today, forcing him to take up residence in tomorrow. As a consequence, every engagement he makes can never be honoured. He is always late, and wakes up in the morning with a terrible sense of guilt and failure. When he saw me outside the tailor's, he recognised a kindred spirit, he tells me.

I tell him that he is quite mistaken: I may be renowned for my lateness, but I have been on time on occasion, and no one has stolen my today. This visibly disappoints the man in the dark suit, and he makes his apologies and shuffles off, out of the bar. I am left feeling a little guilty, but I reassure myself that there is nothing to feel bad about.

That night, I am seized with the idea that someone has stolen my today. I find, the next day, that I have missed all my appointments by twenty-four hours.

At siesta, I see a man in a dark suit greeting an acquaintance with a firm handshake and a smile. I overhear the words 'Glad you could make it.'

Shears

I make a daring escape from a maximum-security prison camp, and, after effecting my egress from the moist tunnel, plunge headlong into the trunky darkness of the pine forests that encircle these regions.

I scramble beneath the needled branches for some time before I realise I have a pair of garden shears embedded in my stomach, the weathered handles protruding in the direction of my escape. I attempt to wrench them from my flesh, but the pain is too great. Reluctantly I leave the shears in my belly, and stumble onwards.

With deepening anxiety, I become slowly aware that, with each step, the blades of the shears move infinitesimally closer, cutting into something vital that is deep inside me.

I have no choice but to continue, and as dusk cloaks the forests I finally emerge into the open plains. I climb, with panting breaths, a ridge and stand there, horribly conscious, gazing towards a dubious future. The shears are almost closed.

PHLEGM

Wage Packet

During a period of poverty more pronounced than usual I consider applying for a job. A concerned friend suggests that I try for a place at the restaurant where she was, until recently, employed as a waitress. The most usual position to come up is that of dishwasher. My friend warns me that dishwashers are considered the lowest of the low, an underpaid subclass treated abominably. She tells me that in a restaurant there is a structured hierarchy of abuse; the owner harangues the manager, who insults the chef, who turns angrily on the preparation staff, who vent spleen on the waiting staff, who then unleash their fury on the dishwasher. The dishwasher has very little room for manoeuvre in this concatenation of spite. I assure my friend that I will be fine, and ask her for directions to the restaurant. The chances are that I will not need the job, that something will turn up.

A week later my financial situation has not improved, so I take a bath, put on some relatively clean clothes and walk to the restaurant. The manager cannot see me as he is 'off sick', but after a lengthy wait I am summoned to the office, where the assistant manager introduces herself to me. The office is small, and smells of things that I cannot identify. She asks me why I want the job. I say I had always wanted a career in catering. She asks me if I have any experience, and I reply that I am keen to learn. She wants to know if I work well as a team member, whether I am what she refers to as a 'people person' and also whether I have any prior convictions. After a passing reference to the conduct expected of her employees, she outlines my responsibilities and the hours I will be required to work.

I ask her if that means I have got the job, and she answers that she will be in touch. I leave the restaurant with mixed feelings. On the one hand, I think I dealt with the interview quite well. However, I failed to get the last job I applied for, and that was only to work as a shelf stacker – or, rather, replenishment operative – at a down-market superstore near the ring road. But essentially I feel positive about my prospects.

Three days later I receive a telephone call from the assistant manager. She enquires about the possibility of my working in the kitchens that evening. I ask her if that means I have got the job, and she answers that we will have to see how things go. This evening's work will be both a 'trial period' and a 'training session'. I want to know if I will be paid for the work, and she tells me that 'training periods' are not paid. In fact, she adds, with something of a giggle in her voice, perhaps I should pay for this training. I laugh sycophantically and put the phone down. The sky outside begins to rain, and I look around my room, as if for the last time.

The restaurant is very busy. There is a queue outside, and the waiters and waitresses look harassed. I am hustled through the dining area to the kitchen, which I see houses two red-faced, angry chefs, three furious prep staff, and two large unattended sinks piled high with dirty dishes and pans.

My 'training session' involves a great deal of washing up. The clientele of this particular restaurant seem to make a lot of mess, and appear to delight in stubbing cigarettes out in their unwanted burgers, fried eggs, prawn cocktails and pork chops. I am also introduced to The Pig, which isn't a pig but rather a large metal machine. The Pig is kept in the very back room of the restaurant, along with large empty metal tins that once contained cooking oil and empty cardboard boxes. I pour food scraps scraped from plates into a bucket, which I then tip sloppily into one end of The Pig. I press a green button, and The Pig shakes and emits a terrible noise made of crushing bones and churning matter. When the noise subsides and the food scraps are all gone I press a red button, and The Pig shudders to a halt. Then I return to the sinks and try to catch up with the piles of crockery that have accumulated during my time away.

By the end of the evening I am very tired, but the assistant manager calls me aside, and she insists that I join her and some of the waiters for what turns out to be four hours of lager and a great many cigarettes. We all agree that the catering business is a tough business that attracts people who are the 'salt of the earth'. I feel very agreeable when I finally get home, and I fall asleep easily, dreaming only of detergent and the sound The Pig makes as it digests the leftovers.

In the morning I feel considerably less sanguine. When I remember that I agreed last night to a shift at the restaurant starting at one o'clock I groan loudly and slump back into my bed. I realise that I worked for six hours and have nothing except a headache. Outside the sky is raining again and the seagulls are mocking me.

At around half past one I walk through the dining area to the room at the back. The assistant manager looks very cross, and tells me that she will be docking my wages because of my lateness. She asks me if I have 'punctuality issues'. I say that I have not, and ask her how she can dock wages that I don't have. This is the wrong thing to say.

Later, when I am called upon to clean out the pork buckets, I realise my headache has subsided. The job in hand is, however, so thoroughly nauseating and dispiriting that I take advantage of a lull in the restaurant's activity to step outside for some fresh air. The assistant manager joins me and offers me a cigarette. She begins to tell me that she isn't really a bitch and when she was a little girl she wanted to be a ballerina. Because the fucking manager is 'off sick' she has to do all the fucking work and really she wants a quiet life in a cottage in the country. It would be different if she was the manager. For a start she would be able to afford a better car and a better house. I sympathise, and then decide to take advantage of her mood and ask about my wages. She glares furiously at me, asserts that I drank them last night, had the temerity to turn up late on the busiest day of the week, and adds that the only reason she hasn't sacked me already is because she is a good person and is determined to give me a chance.

During this interlude both of the sinks have filled with plates and cutlery, and wearily I begin to empty one sink so I can fill it with water and detergent. After scraping the plates free of unwanted food and greasy cigarette butts I take the now-full bucket to The Pig. I press the green button, and feed The Pig with something approaching tenderness. Soon I will be forced to share its diet. I can see myself squirrelling choice leftovers into my pockets to be devoured later, out of sight of the rest of the staff.

Eventually the last customers leave the restaurant, meaty arms draped around one another. My chores keep me busy for another half an hour, and when I hang up my apron and head for the door I am stopped by the assistant manager and invited to share a table with her and three waiters, one of the chefs and two of the food-preparation staff. I protest, saying that I cannot afford to spend any more of my wages on lager. They look confused, until the assistant manager says something quietly to them, whereupon they burst out laughing. It seems that the assistant manager was only joking with me about that particular matter. The lager is a perk of the job, a fringe benefit. It occurs to me that to have a fringe you ideally need a main event, such as a wage, for the benefit to be attached to. However, I am too tired to mention it, and drink lager for several hours. The assistant manager may have wanted to be a ballerina, but the chef had always dreamt of a career in the army, two of the waiters were actually 'resting' between acting jobs, the third intended to be a comedian, and the food preppers both intended to become property developers.

The night ends in raucous laughter, toasts to the 'salt of the earth' (ourselves) and jokes about how ill we will all feel in the morning. I stumble home through the rain, thinking generous thoughts about my co-workers, and eventually fall into a sleep filled with dreams about the glutinous matter that stubbornly adheres to the bottom of the pork buckets.

I am awoken from my gritty sofa by a determined hammering on the front door. It is my landlord, who wishes to collect the last two weeks' rent. I clutch at my temples and tell him about my new job. This seems to assuage his incipient fury, as long as I pay him as soon as I get my wages, and he leaves, muttering dark threats about bailiffs. This morning, I realise, will not be productive. I trudge up to bed, anxious to sleep the remaining hours until my one o'clock shift begins.

I make pains to arrive on time, and the assistant manager nods curtly at me as I don my apron. I know for certain that I am extremely hungry, but the leftovers I scrape into the bucket repel me, coated as they are in cold, coagulated grease and studded with crushed cigarette butts. I ask the chef who wanted to join the army if I can have a burger. He flips one over and passes it to me on a metal spatula, warning me that it will 'have to come out of my wages'. I am not sure if he is joking or not, and he turns his red face back to the griddle before I can ask him.

The burger is still pink and raw at its core, but I eat it rapidly, feeling a surge of energy almost immediately. I redouble my vigour with the dishes and pans, and before long the bucket is full of waste food. I go to feed The Pig, and it gurgles as I feed it. I have saved the leftover desserts for last, and The Pig lets out a contented belching sound as I pour in melted Knickerbocker Glories. But then there is a terrible sound of grinding, a shrieking, shearing noise that fills me with alarm. Hastily I press the red button, and The Pig judders on the concrete floor before falling silent. For a minute or two I stand still, the empty bucket in one hand, the other hand hovering a few inches away from The Pig.

When I tell the chef who wanted to join the army what has happened he too stands motionless for a short time. Then he turns to face me, shaking his head, and says that I'd better go and tell the manager. I remind him that the manager is 'off sick'. He says that I had better tell the assistant manager, then. Still shaking his head, he returns to the griddle. With trepidation I leave the kitchens and wait in the busy dining area until the assistant manager notices me. She walks rapidly towards me, flicking her finger to remind me of my grease-smeared clothing and generally unkempt appearance, and she mouths unfriendly words. The force of her personality pushes me back through the door into the kitchen, where she stands very close to me and asks me what exactly do I mean by barging into the dining area like that. I explain the dreadful noise that The Pig made, and she marches through to the back room, with me scurrying at her heels. She presses the green button, and again The Pig makes that hideous screaming noise. The assistant manager presses the red button and turns to me, her eyes narrow slits, her face red, her whole body shaking slightly. I find difficult to imagine that this woman could ever have dreamt of tutus and ballet pumps. I picture her in them, and release an involuntary smile with my mouth. This is the wrong thing to do. The screaming that comes from the assistant manager is even worse than that which came from The Pig, which was at least non-verbal. She calls me a great many names, implies that my brain is retarded and that I am impotent, that my penis is smaller than her little finger. It seems that I have inadvertently fed The Pig a piece of cutlery. This will do terrible things to the grinders, she says. She tells me that because she is only the fucking assistant manager she cannot sanction calling in the fucking mechanic. I ask if we can't telephone the manager and ask him to sanction it, but she spits furiously at me that he. Is. Off. Sick. And then she tells me I now have to empty the buckets of scraps into the empty cooking-oil cans, and she storms off, to get back to some real work and away from fucking imbeciles such as myself. Oh, and the damage to The Pig, when it has been costed, will come out of my wages.

This is bad. The empty oil cans are quite large, but after three shifts here I know how much waste is fed to The Pig. There are only about twenty of the oil cans in the room, and I calculate that they will be full after the end of this evening. But there is nothing I can do. I am in disgrace in the kitchen. Nobody speaks to me, and I tend to the sinks, washing dishes, drying cutlery and so on until the prepping staff wordlessly push the pork buckets across the floor to me. On my trips to the back room The Pig sits idle while I pour the slops into the cooking-oil cans. The room begins to smell quite abominable, and I worry that the ghastly odour of the intermingled food waste will drift through the dining area, getting me into even more trouble. I wedge open the top window, hoping that the smell will be drawn out into the night air.

After work I am not invited to drink lager with the others, and make my way home disconsolately through the rain. I have no food at home, and nothing to drink except tap water. I sit for a while looking out of the window, and then suddenly I have an idea.

I leave the house, and walk briskly. The rain has stopped, and although it is still very windy the sky is clearing, and stars are visible through the orange haze of the city. In the alley which the restaurant backs onto I see that the top window of the back room is still wedged open, as I left it. I find a crate and stand on it, reaching through to unlatch the larger part of the window. Once inside, I close the window and turn on the light. Any hopes I might have had of salvaging something to eat from the oil cans are immediately quashed by the foul state of the mess within them. Then I realise: of course! The kitchen is full of food. I can help myself! Once in the kitchen I help myself to several prawn cocktails, a salad and some of the burger buns. I look longingly at the frozen burgers and decide to try to turn the griddle on. I place several frozen burgers on the bars, figuring that what I cannot eat now I can take home with me.

Suddenly I feel quite full, and sit outstretched on the floor. Then I begin to feel guilty. If the assistant manager finds out about this I will be quite done for. Not only will I get the sack without even having got paid, I will actually owe money for breaking The Pig. By now the food must be sustaining my mental faculties, for I have another brainwave.

In the back room I find a spanner, and study The Pig. It looks as if I can remove the side plate, which should reveal the inner workings. I am not of a mechanical bent, but I reason that it should be relatively easy to locate the errant piece of cutlery and extricate it somehow from the grinders. So I kneel to undo the bolts on the side panel and work it free from its housing. And then, in a gusting rush, a tide of revolting slop shoots out of The Pig, drenching me and spreading rapidly in a noisome flood all over the floor. The stench is atrocious, and without being able to stop myself I vomit copiously again and again, desperately crawling backwards through the filth on my hands and knees away from the still-flowing river of macerated burgers, egg, bread, prawns, cigarette butts, pork and various accompanying dishes.

I reach the wall opposite and haul myself into a standing position. I am now dry retching, and my first meal in some time is mingling with the lake of effluent at my feet. As I try frantically to work out what to do, I hear a roar from the kitchen. The griddle! I wade through the disgusting goo to the kitchen door and push it open, inadvertently allowing the backed-up sludge to pour through. To my horror the entire griddle area under the extraction hood seems to be on fire, my burgers barely visible through the flames. Without hesitating I splash back and grab the bucket, scooping up about half a gallon of slop from the floor, and rush back into the kitchen to fling it at the griddle. To my relief the flames die back a little, so I repeat the exercise several times more until the fire is completely out. I stand there, the empty bucket dangling from my hand, surveying the full horror of the situation. I have never seen anything even remotely as disgusting as the scene before me.

I tell myself that this is impossible. How can a long-handled teaspoon from a Knickerbocker Glory glass have caused this devastation? The kitchen and back room are flooded with the foulest liquid imaginable, the griddle and the walls adjacent to it are splattered and flecked with the same, the griddle itself is probably beyond repair, and I myself am covered almost head to toe in mashed, rotting leftovers and my own vomit. The smell is horrendous, and I cannot help but notice that the flood is seeping into the dining area under the swing doors that separate it from the kitchen. And, of course, The Pig is still broken.

I cannot stand it. I am incapable of anything except escape. I leave, slamming the back door behind me. The wind has stopped, and with every step the stench wafts up to my nostrils. Eventually I get home, and with incredible relief turn on the shower, peel off my sodden clothes and stuff them into the bin. I stand under the shower for what could be hours, then dry myself and fall into bed, and then into sleep.

In the morning it takes a while for the gravity of my predicament to sink in. I cannot decide what to do, and the fact that I am afflicted with a ravenous hunger does not make clear thought any easier. At last I decide to turn up for work at one o'clock as normal, and feign complete ignorance of what has happened to the restaurant.

When I arrive I am considerably disconcerted to find the premises cordoned off with police incident tape. The staff are huddled outside, talking urgently, and I walk over, and innocently enquire about what has happened. The waiter who intends to become a comedian tells me that the restaurant is now a murder scene. He says that the early shift arrived to find the place in complete disarray, that there had been a fire, and something like a burst sewer pipe had flooded the ground floor. It had been the sanitising contractors who had raised the alarm when they found what they thought were human finger bones in the sewage. The police had arrived, and sealed the building with blue-and-white tape. No one was allowed in.

Overcome with conflicting emotions I walk a short distance away and sit down on the pavement. Human finger bones? It is all rather too much. After the trauma of the previous night I cannot take this new development in. I have to eat something. I walk back over to my colleagues and broach the subject of our wages, and what is likely to happen now that there will be no work at this establishment for some time, or, more likely, ever. The other chef, the one whose aspirations I am unaware of, tells me that there is little chance of getting paid now. No one has been able to contact the manager, and in any case it is doubtful, even if he were to arrive, that the police would allow access to the safe.

I'm not feeling very good. I leave, and then remember my friend, the one who recommended that I get a job at this restaurant. I walk over to her house, and she lets me in, looking very concerned and asking if I'm all right. I answer that I'm not, not really, and recount my awful experiences since I last saw her. And I ask her if she has any food.

After eating a sandwich and drinking a brandy I'm beginning to feel a little clearer. My friend has heard about the murder/restaurant business on the radio. I ask her if she thinks that I will be a suspect, because I must have left fingerprints all over the place last night. She doesn't think so; she tells me that all the staff will have done the same. And in any case, she says that the radio said that the police are treating the disappearance of the restaurant's manager as 'suspicious'. Apparently he first went 'off sick' when she was still working there, and no one has seen him since that time. I ask for another sandwich.

We listen to the radio, but apart from what the Chief Superintendent calls 'significant developments' and an 'ongoing investigation' nothing much has happened. The corpse has been partly reassembled and 'is thought to be a male in his mid-to-late forties', which my friend tells me fits the description of the manager. I think of The Pig, and those bone-crunching sounds it made. I had almost come to feel affection for it, but now my feelings are more of revulsion. The fact that I have been sprayed with the decomposed and macerated remains of the manager makes me feel quite horrible. We get the brandy out again and I'm afraid that I drink most of it.

At six we turn on the television set to watch the news, but I am a little too drunk to focus on it properly. I fall into a doze, but my friend wakes me by shaking my shoulder. The television screen swims into view, and I watch with shock as I see the assistant manager, screaming in a most familiar way, being manhandled into the back of a police van, lashing out and spitting at the police. The reporter announces that she has been arrested on suspicion of murder, then tells the viewers how it is alleged that she dismembered the manager and fed him to The Pig, which the reporter refers to as a 'waste-disposal unit'. It further transpires that she has been raiding his bank accounts to make a deposit on a rural property and to invest in a prestigious ballet academy.

I am astounded. I feel almost like an accomplice, especially when I think of The Pig. I think I am in some sort of shock. I fall asleep again.

When I awaken it is the morning, and my friend has gone to work. She has left me a note, saying that I can stay there and to help myself to anything in the kitchen. I trudge desultorily to the refrigerator and drink some milk. I realise with a dreadful empty feeling that I still have no money. There is a local paper in the sitting room, and I sit on the sofa, leafing through the 'situations vacant' pages, imagining what appalling horror will befall me when I next try to earn a wage.

Sell Your House and Buy Gold

There was disaster coming; that was obvious. Life had been almost ridiculously easy, and now things were going to get worse. Much, much worse. I couldn't believe that I had ever thought otherwise. I couldn't believe that I'd ever thought that there could be any other outcome.

But I had.

I had disregarded a thousand different types and variations of warning for years.

I had believed implicitly in the power of the Authorities to deal with any situation that may have worried me.

My bookshelves were full of books, packed with scientific explanations, and I had taken out a variety of insurance that implied my life was worth money.

I did not think that my life or, more precisely, the manner in which I lived it was effectively an inexorably lengthy suicide, although, of course, it was.

Small things were changing, but I had preferred to remain oblivious.

I did not much miss the butterflies, and birdsong had only reminded me of mobile phones or car alarms anyway.

Disaster I thought of in inverted commas:

'DISASTER'.

It was something that, if it were to happen, would look

like extremely expensive special effects.

Because the world was big, and seemed to alter only in the details, I slowly became comfortable in many assumptions. I fossilised into what I saw as an eternally stable sediment.

In this state I engaged actively with property, clothing, money, culture, and had a vested interest in continuing to do so.

In this I was not alone.

Even though I had often observed newly born swarms of mayflies smashed to pieces by a sudden and unexpected showers of hailstones, I often used credit cards.

Even though I myself had mercilessly crushed legions of ants beneath my feet, I took out a mortgage on a house that I then renovated, decorated and bought furniture for. And even though I had seen on the television many harbingers of disaster, I carried on acting as if nothing was wrong.

All of this was an error.

No. Not just an error; it was an immense mistake.

When, at last and unequivocally, I had to admit to my deeply comfortable self that disaster really was coming and that its coming was inevitable, I took certain steps.

Everyone that I knew of lived in houses, and it rapidly became clear that all of these houses were either too old, too dangerously situated, or in any number of other ways inappropriate. We used our diverse and highly developed skills to research the question of what to do.

We decided to build a new house that had none of the drawbacks of previous habitats. We selected a site and had the house built. The disaster was definitely coming, but money still worked as it always had, as did credit, mortgages, property, and all the other things we clothed ourselves with.

There seemed to be no particular urgency regarding the disaster; only a dull sort of inevitability. Our new house fulfilled all the requirements we sought, but there was one thing we had not thought about.

One thing we had not got right.

We built a house with too many shadows in it. It wasn't the sort of thing that you notice at first; oh no.

The shadows did not become evident until it was too late.

Of course. Not until it was much, much too late.

And soon it was clear to us all that the disaster was almost upon us. This we deduced from the undeniable fact that many of the things to which we had become accustomed began to stop functioning.

The telephones became unreliable, and there was often no money in the holes in the walls. There was no more petrol, which led to some very unpleasant scenes, both on the roads and elsewhere. People had certainly been guilty of selfishness before, but the stoppage of petrol made a lot of people act extremely thoughtlessly.

In addition to our frequent and increasing daily troubles, the always-awkward-to-reach call-centre employees whom we relied upon for many things were frequently completely absent, and when the telephone systems did actually work we were usually rebuffed by recorded voices that enticed us through several options before becoming silent.

One evening the television had nothing to show us.

And then, almost suddenly, it was no longer possible to buy newspapers, or indeed many sundries including soap, dish-washing tablets, razors, light bulbs, vacuum-cleaner bags or toilet paper, as the family who had owned the shop had gone. We tried to find other shops, but the families who owned them had gone too.

We now had to think about the how of getting, rather than the how much to get. This was a strain. It occurred to me, not infrequently, that our civilisation had, of late, begun to make the simplest things extremely tortuous. We had perfected what now seemed a psychotic level of complexity around simple human activities like eating, keeping clean, and moving from one place to another.

Our supply of electricity became erratic. At the end of a day filled with minor panics of one sort or another it was apparent that there was no more of it at all.

That was where our real problems started.

Looking back, I can see that they began long before that. Our problems began a long, long time ago, when they were invisible, and continued during their gradual appearance.

The problems grew and were nurtured by our casual indifference, our sneers, and the ignorant manner in which we chose to live. Our gestating problems were the dark, inevitable spectre that accompanied us to the cash-point, into work, to the supermarket, and into our gritty, tortured beds.

And after the end of the electricity, the shadows conspired against us.

The dark corners began to scare us more than the coming disaster. The disaster was imminent; that was clear from the disappearance of many things that we had assumed to be vital to our being. But the threat from the shifting shadows in our house was worse, far worse.

We began, almost imperceptibly, to panic.

However much we reassured ourselves that we were safe, that the disaster would flow over us, that we had stockpiled, that we were defended and guarded against every eventuality, the insistent shadows illuminated our vulnerability.

When night came, we fell to a brooding quietude, eyeing each other with suspicion, inventing justifications for our dark feelings.

We cloaked our hidden desires; we conspired with the shadows.

Nothing seemed to be happening.

*

The television, I realised, had been a sort of terminal that connected me to a wider understanding of events. And without newspapers it was impossible not to write my own internal headlines during my sleepless nights. Worry became constant; worry and enforced exile from everything I was accustomed to.

I had never envisaged a sort of loneliness that did not involve people. But in fact it was the lack of small items that I had previously taken for granted that made me lonely. I missed tea, toothpaste, remote controls, coffee, ballpoint pens, margarine, AA batteries, and easy credit in high-street stores. I missed my favourite magazines.

And the dead silence that encloaked the telephone and the television made me lonely. And the hollow look in the eyes of the people – oh . . .

After the end of electricity, the nights lengthened.

We had to wait in the dark, listening.

Life had quickly become intolerable for some of us.

It wasn't that I found my existence more tolerable than theirs; only that I felt that I had a sort of fortitude, a sort of – wisdom.

Nobody was happy.

The light in the house became less and less; the shadows darker and darker.

Still we waited for the disaster.

★

And when I looked, when people moved in front of the windows in the grey light, their shadows cast quickly clattering dark talons across the floor. This only became worse as the light faded.

I forbade them from moving, as it had become impossible to tell shadow from shadow. Or shadow from human.

Mine was a necessary act, an act that intended to prove that we had to be strong and united against the looming disaster.

The man had always been unreliable, but certain events had proved to me that he was a liability. If it had not been me it would have been another who would have had to take that awful decision.

Nobody witnessed anything; not that it would have made any difference if they had.

I was not ashamed, and after a certain amount of uproar I explained my reasoning and my actions to the others. But I did not go into the details; if I had told them about his struggling, and how long it took, there would undoubtedly have been problems.

We carried his carcass beyond the perimeter wire and left it in a ditch.

Inevitably, there were people who objected, and they were next.

When disaster is coming it is difficult to see clearly, but somehow I could see through the shadows to the light.

A long period of unpleasantness followed.

*

As the people in the house became fewer the shadows seemed to increase in number and in density. Often I perused my fading bank statements, lost in a reverie of long-gone financial transactions. I disliked being disturbed. Yes. I disliked that.

The disaster was coming. That was clear.

There were shadows everywhere.

When I was at last alone, when the people were all gone, I waited for the disaster on my own.

On my own.

My Giro

I was in a dreadful situation. The Department had got me. Usually I had been able to avoid these situations by earnestly prevaricating, feigning excitement at a new 'project' that I was certain would lead me to a paradise in which my Giro would be nothing but a faint memory. Never before had they tricked me into actually accepting a position of work.

Looking back, I should have known it. The man smiled at me, allowing no ambiguity about the way the corners of his eyes crinkled. I was ready for the usual questions, but I hesitated when he asked me if he was right in thinking I was an artist. I made an almost silent flopping noise with my tongue as he went on to tell me that he had 'just the thing' for me.

I had the horrible sensation that I was taking part in the tortured dream of some sort of prisoner. I felt a morbid chill low in my insides.

The man was almost gleeful as he opened a file and passed a piece of A4 paper into my hand. I listened to him saying something, but his words had no meaning. He may as well have been speaking Latin. I looked at the piece of paper. I was led to a small room. Somehow there was a biro, and somehow I was sitting down signing the piece of A4 paper, and my mind seemed very far away, and I listened to the crackle and fizz of the static that erupted from the carpet.

And suddenly I was walking down the concrete steps to the street and I was employed. I had a job.

The job was, apparently, in a tattoo shop in a surprisingly smart part of the town. There were people, employed people, everywhere, all looking as if they needed to be somewhere other than where they were at that instant, apart from those who sat in the many restaurants that lined the streets. They looked as if they had been born to dine in precisely those restaurants. A wave of nausea coursed through me.

I sat on a bench between two saplings, and stared at the dust between my feet. I sank my face into my hands and began to moan quietly.

What was I going to do? I had to take the job. If I didn't take the job, or if I got the sack, or if I left, I was fucked. The Department wouldn't give me any more money. I either had to be made redundant, in which case the Department would reluctantly pay me my fortnightly allowance, or I had to become some sort of criminal, a life for which I lacked many fundamental skills.

I had to take the job. I had no choice.

After some time had passed, I got up and walked to the shop and introduced myself, mentioned the Department, and handed over the piece of A4 paper. I made my mouth move into some approximate smiles, and expressed a dull sort of keenness. My keenness was, however, overshadowed by the enthusiasm of the two managers of the shop. They explained excitedly that the franchise was an entirely new concept in tattoo parlours, in that the tattoos already existed and were grafted onto the recipient. The tattoos were carefully sliced from the bodies of corpses, young corpses being preferable as the artwork would not have blurred and turned blue.

The corpses were stored in a refrigerated chamber at the back of the shop, where they lay stiffly, awaiting a wealthy customer who would take their illustrated skin for their own.

I thought back to the morning, when I had awoken at 10.30 and ambled across the town to sign on at the Department.

That life now seemed distant.

My tasks at the shop were not onerous, but I desperately missed my indolence. I was required to be at work early in the morning, when the streets were filled with strange smells and sounds I was unaccustomed to. At the shop I sat behind a desk and, when a customer entered, would talk vaguely with them, correlating their personal details with entries in a database. I saw the managers in the morning and at closing time, and at lunchtime they would leave the premises to dine in one of the restaurants.

I was not so lucky. The interruption of my routine had unbalanced my eating habits severely. A gnawing, acidic hunger plagued my belly, but the idea of eating my hastily prepared packed lunches was completely repellent. Consequently I began to focus unhealthily on what I imagined took place in the back rooms when the managers were working on the customers. During slack periods I would stare with unfocused eyes at the computer monitor, images of scalpels and the dark blood on green latex gloves washing against the shores of my mind.

I also thought often of Giros I had cashed in the past, each one like a beautiful girlfriend who had been everything I wanted, but whom I had never really appreciated. I hadn't much cared for the Department, but from my chair behind my desk, behind the plate glass that glazed the shop, my memories grew fonder.

The idea of the tattoo grafts disgusted me. There was no art needed here. Despite what had been said to me, this was definitely not 'just the thing for me'. I wanted desperately to be made redundant.

After several weeks the managers asked me if I would like a promotion. The franchise was going well, and one of the managers was going to open a shop in the next town. They were going to hire a new receptionist, and offered me a position on the team.

Darkly, in a gloomy corner of my being, I clutched at my Giro, but it was further out of my reach than ever. Somehow, a piece of A4 paper and a biro had altered my life profoundly. I had no idea how to undo the alteration.

It was growing dark outside, and I was led into a room that was artificially lit.

There was much to learn, and at first it didn't seem possible that I would ever be on the team. But the manager who had remained at the shop persevered, and eventually his sometimes-manic enthusiasm paid off.

An effect of the arrangement that I had not considered was my increased wage. Startled, I moved to a nicer flat, and began to take an interest in shop-window displays. At lunchtime I went to restaurants with the manager who had remained at the shop and I developed an interest in dining that was wholly new to me. It was only occasionally now that I felt hunger, and those times were like a dimly felt nostalgia.

I bought a bicycle, and at weekends I cycled out of the town to hills in the countryside where I would grunt and sweat my way to a summit, and there survey the land spread before me. Birds sang strange tunes in the trees, and the clouds formed distant plateaux.

The corpses never stayed on the premises for longer than was necessary. I surprised myself daily with the corpses. I learned how to push down gently with a scalpel until the skin gently popped and I was able to slice through the skin, bisecting freckles, drawing a straight line that curved acutely as I changed direction. Once the tattoo was encircled I lifted one edge and attached the clamps. The patch of illustrated epidermis came away relatively easily, needing few nicks and cuts at subcutaneous matter with the scalpel.

I developed a taste for Italian food, and gradually became known as a high-tipping regular at one of the restaurants. My favourite table, by the window, was always made available for me.

The summer drew on, and a thick, sultry heat settled on the town. I no longer used my bicycle since I found that I was arriving at work with dark circles of sweat under the arms of my shirts, which quickly grew uncomfortable in the air-conditioned office.

I bought a car after learning to drive one. I found learning difficult, as there were three distinct pedals, a steering wheel, a gearstick, several mirrors, windscreen wipers, indicators, different sorts of lights, and a complex dashboard featuring more dials than I could hope to decipher. And, of course, there was a windscreen, the view from which required constant monitoring.

However, I eventually overcame these difficulties, and was able to drive to work in the same state of forgetful bewilderment I was sure I shared with my fellow commuters.

I still sometimes thought about my Giro, but the numbers printed in the little rectangle on the right were indistinct and smudged, and I could not quite make out the amount.

After all, I had been able to forget most of my girlfriends.

When I had been at the shop for about a year I was in the novel position of manager. I had both a professional and, to a lesser extent, a personal authority over two key workers who I referred to as my team, and two receptionists, one of whom also worked as my secretary.

In the morning I would look through the photographs of tattoos that had been emailed to me, choosing those which I considered would be quickly resold, or that were particularly artistic and would fetch higher premiums. Most of the surgery (or 'hackwork', as we in the team referred privately to it) was now undertaken by my colleagues, but I still preferred to handle particularly large or prestigious pieces.

After choosing that day's purchases and authorising money transfers, I tended to spend an hour or so with my money, moving it from one place to another, in a manner that resembled a ghost playing Patience. I had never seen my money, but I was reassured by the sequences of digits on my computer screen and drew pleasure from watching them increase.

At lunchtime I would walk to my usual restaurant. I had tried almost everything that had ever been on the menu, but my favourite remained spaghetti Bolognese, and my white napkin caught splatters of salsa di pomodoro as I ate.

The afternoons were largely occupied with administrative matters. I was now comfortable with A4 paper, but as biros still nagged at a haunted attic of my mind I preferred to use my computer and printing machine, signing letters with a fountain pen.

Quite often I would spend the evening with the receptionist who also worked as my secretary. We had sex in my new flat, where she would attach me to my bed with ties and belts before taking my erect penis into various parts of herself.

For a few frightened moments after my orgasm had subsided I worried that she would refuse to untie me, and I would be found by archaeologists of the future on the rusting iron springs of my bed, my flesh mummified on my emaciated frame.

★

I now regularly bought newspapers, and felt comforted by the vast prairies of knowledge that I had assimilated. Often I would dispute political matters in restaurants and at the dinner parties I attended. Frequently I found myself with words falling from my mouth that I barely recognised, but as they met with approval or enthusiasm I did not worry much.

At night, when I was not fucking my secretary, I would spend many hours in the passenger seat of my car, looking out of the window at the interior of my garage, which shimmered in my eyes, my bicycle shadowed on the bricks, interrogated by the fluorescent striplight.

More time passed, and I was being paid considerably more money whilst actually having less to do. I now often visited other people's offices, and they often visited mine. I became adept at handling biros, A4 paper, and the use of argument and persuasion. I was pleased that many meetings proved successful if held in restaurants, particularly if we all got drunk.

I decided to extend the franchise overseas, and asked my people to arrange it. This happened easily, without my having to alter my habits very much. I found air travel less harrowing than I had first imagined, as I had a propensity for queuing.

Deluges of A4 paper were used in a deft manoeuvring of intangible properties, and the numbers I surveyed on my computer screen grew laterally. I was now rich, and wondered what my face would look like in photographs.

★

And then my life fell into small pieces. The letter from the Department was delivered, after being redirected four times, to my new offices. I was choosing the paint, but the subtleties of green were forgotten when I recognised the logo on the envelope. I requested that the interior designer should go away by making a gesture I had copied from television. With shaking fingers I opened the envelope and pulled from it a piece of A4 paper, folded twice.

It generically congratulated me on my new job, and had a computer-printed signature. There was also a questionnaire to fill in. *Was I happy in my new employment?*

I dropped the piece of paper, and stood in my new office, a wealthy and successful man. Something immensely sad passed through my mind, my Giro fluttering for ever out of my reach.

I walked a little way and sat down on a bench between two saplings, and stared at the dust between my feet. I sank my face into my hands and began to moan quietly.

Here Be Dragons

I was somewhere south of somewhere, north of somewhere else, east of everywhere and west of nowhere at all. I had been wandering along endlessly straight roads and tracks that dissected peroxide-bright prairies of barley, which the wind lashed into yellow oceans on which long, low, black ships sailed with their unseen slave cargo of caged poultry.

I'd made some kind of mistake, I now knew. I had begun with the idea that my world – encircled and delineated by diaries, deadlines, telephones, newspapers, emails, bank statements, bills, invoices, tax demands, mortgage payments – might be a creation merely of my own. Perhaps simply by removing myself from this apparently scripted existence I could discover a species of reality that had been previously invisible to my blinkered senses.

In some ways I wished myself in an era when the known had faded at the edges, where civilisation petered out into blank spaces occupied with the superstition of the unknown: here be dragons. But England had long been charted in exhaustive detail by Ordnance Survey maps; maps that showed every building, each gradient, each brook and pond, every pylon. Useful, doubtlessly, but also somehow imprisoning.

And what happened was this: browsing the Ordnance Survey map section in a bookshop one morning, I had first been annoyed and then intrigued by the absence of a certain sheet number. I crossed town to another bookshop. It wasn't there either. To be certain, I checked at the library, where it was also missing. I began to feel excited. More than anything, I wanted to be off the map. I imagined the roads becoming track-like, sketched roughly over the terrain like tangled spider silk. I saw trees larger, hedges wilder, the shapes of distant mountains torn against a perfect sky. Above all I saw no people, no animals, and no birds.

I studied the map of the area just to the south of the empty zone where I determined to stake my nebulous claim. And I resolved to travel there.

By train, bus and walking I took myself to the top of this sheet. There was no road north, just a brambled gap in the hedge. I pushed through the clinging stems and looked north with a broad smile. I had told no one where I was going.

I walked for a long time.

Later, much later, I began to worry if I was anywhere at all. I had no idea when I would reach somewhere with a railway station. Or a bus station. Or a bus stop. Or a minicab office. It became so quiet I hoped for a jet to split the mocking sky. That evening I travelled into what seemed a kinder landscape; the lanes began to meander and sink between hedges as the sun sank lower and the air cooled.

My rucksack was heavy and painful on my sunburnt shoulders, and it was clear that I would soon have to find somewhere to put up my tent. At the brow of a gentle decline I saw ahead of me a dark wood massing about a mile distant. It was there, I decided, I would spend the night. The wood began at a fork in the lane where a small cottage lay beneath the purpling shade of the twilit trees. At the gate stood what I thought was a man, bent with age, holding a scythe upright, the blade swinging idly above his head.

I walked on, into the chilly shadows of the trees that grew along one side of the lane. I walked until I was out of view before I lurched off the road into the wood. I squeezed through the shrubbish undergrowth, picked my way through a head-high tangle of brambles, and found myself alone in the wood. It was the most silent wood I have ever been in. It gave the impression of being dead, despite the verdant appearance it had given from outside. The dense leaves of the wood had been forced skywards by the burgeoning deadness of its interior. The expired leaves and twigs beneath my feet cracked like chicken bones. There were no birds. There was nothing here.

Yes, I'd made some kind of mistake. I was here by mistake. I knew this with a certainty that was shattering. But night was irreversible, my situation was irreversible. I could do nothing except unpack my tent, erect it, and crawl inside. I couldn't do anything except that. I couldn't sleep, I couldn't think of anything except the distant, faded sound of a stone sharpening a blade. I thought I heard or I heard chicken bones snapping and a rusty gate that creaked painfully on its decrepit hinges. I lay in my sleeping bag with my clothes on, with my shoes on, staring straight ahead, defencelessly conscious of the sound of my breath, horribly awake, off the map and out of sight and away from the map.

Silently I begged for the dawn. Trees, skeletal in their naked brittleness, swept down, brushing the fragile canvas of my tent. There was some grotesque sort of distant footfall, or anyway a noise I couldn't account for. And occasionally but always, the slow, sly, shrill cry of the gate, opening and closing impossibly in the cloaking darkness of the dead of the night. Maybe a sound formed itself into the shape of my name, twisted itself and warped its voice into a terrifying parody of my name and of my ideas and of my plans and of my future. Maybe a sound slithered into my tent shaped like footsteps or knife-sharpening or chasing or a hollow realisation of the impossibility of escape. Maybe that's where I still am, cocooned in a flimsy, fabricated defence against what it is that I desire most; a damned region that lies off the map, unpeopled, empty of birds, bereft of animals, where the sky is torn from the land, and where I am caught for ever, desiccating, last week's insect caught in forgotten, dusty spider silk, suspended across a corner of somewhere that will never be visited again.

Peace and Quiet

On a darkening winter evening I sought cover from the rain in a pub on either Fleet Street or High Holborn. I can't remember which. It had been raining incessantly, and I was wet, which was my own fault. I had left my umbrella at home and didn't want to buy a new one. I had spent the day walking around the back streets, unclear about what it was that I was looking for. I stood transfixed outside St John's Gate watching an aeroplane scratching the underside of the shredded clouds. Later, I came upon a dead market; a few hooded figures picking at the skeletons of the stalls, torn polythene struggling to escape with the wind as the rain pasted it to the tarmac. And I stood for some time at Ludgate Circus, staring at the yellow lines drawn as diamonds on the road, hypnotised by the endless passage of black tyres hissing through the rain across them. By this time the scant grey light that had accompanied me on my perambulations was fading, and I was extremely wet. I don't recall which direction I took but, as I say, I ducked into a pub somewhere nearby.

The place was quiet; a warren of rooms, it seemed to me. I peeled my raincoat from myself and eased off my soaked hat. I found a small table next to a gas fire that sputtered warmly below the red 'appliance condemned' sticker, and took out my notebook. I was partway through what was becoming an interminable project that was frustrating me further with every turn that it took. I didn't know if any of these turns were the right ones, or if I was wasting my time.

My soaked clothes began to gently steam by the gas fire in the pub, though I felt cold, chilled deep to my core. I held a biro over my open notebook as I tried to make something useful of the small events of the day. The old walls of the building muffled the traffic's roar, and my thoughts seemed likewise faded. The yellow light from the tasselled shade reflected against the frosted glass in the window. It was a black night outside. The fire continued to wheeze and choke. I looked down at my notebook. *'There will be no Quiet. There will be no Peace.'* My pen was poised above the final full stop. I frowned, unable to remember writing the words. For the first time I gazed around the room. When I had come in I'd thought the small room was empty, but now I saw that a man was sitting at another table, his back to me. He was wearing a cheap-looking chalk-striped suit, with scuffed black patent-leather shoes. Leaning against the wall next to him was an umbrella, water pooling darkly where the ferrule rested on the floor. His greying hair was slicked back from a balding head, and the lines on his face continued round the back of his neck. He was wearing glasses. I realised I was staring, and looked away. Sighing, I closed my notebook and tucked my biro back in my pocket. I wondered if it was still pouring outside. I gazed around the room, seeing wood panelling and a few Victorian fox-hunting prints. The man at the other table had opened a briefcase that he had in front of him on the table. From it he pulled a sheaf of A4 papers, which had what looked like monochrome photocopied passport photographs on them, about nine to a page. There were about four or five lines of what I guessed were details about each person printed under each photo. He shuffled quickly through the papers, as if to count them, then started to look methodically at each. His pen paused a few times over certain of the pictures on each page, but he evidently decided not to mark any of them. The light glinted in the portion of his glasses that I could see, and suddenly I had the uncomfortable feeling that he could see my reflection in them, and that he had noticed that I was looking at him. But he made no sign that he had. He continued to slowly leaf through his papers. Nevertheless, I looked away.

But I couldn't stare at the ceiling for ever, and I had no interest in the fox-hunting prints. I found my eye was drawn back to that shabby man in that small, yellow-lit room. He had begun to spend longer on each page, bending towards the photocopied images, carefully reading whatever it was that was written beneath them. I had finished my drink, and gathered my wet things, about to leave, when I glanced once more at the man. He was closely studying an image on one of his papers. I now felt coldly certain that he had been aware of my scrutiny, and at that moment he turned his lined face towards me, studied me for a moment, nodded slowly and slightly, and mirthlessly smiled. He turned back before circling a photograph with his red pen.

I rushed past his icy presence, bolted from the room, along the passage and out into the cold rain of either High

Holborn or Fleet Street. But not before I had recognised the face in the photograph, and read, unmistakably, my own name beneath it.

Condiment

So one day I began collecting: I urinated into a large jar. I masturbated and scooped my ejaculate into a second jar. I took a knife from the drawer and made an incision on the end of my finger and squeezed the blood in thin trickles and fat drops into a third jar. I sat down with a fourth jar on my lap, and thought of sad things. Then I wept into the jar. I repeated these actions every evening, each fluid into its appointed jar. After a month, I emptied the contents of the jars into small saucepans, which I heated carefully until I had evaporated the liquid. When the pans had cooled, I scraped the residue, with the aid of a funnel, into separate salt cellars. I then tasted each of my personal salts, judging which would go best with what food.

My experiment was a resounding success. The salts seemed to impart a subtle intensity to spicy dishes, and a freshness and zest to even the most homely soup. And so my restaurant began to attract many more patrons as increasing numbers of adulatory reviews appeared in some of the Sunday supplements.

Obviously, I had to continue to produce the salts that had made my culinary creations such overnight successes. My establishment was now being patronised by celebrities as well as politicians and the merely rich.

My difficulty lay chiefly with eliciting sadness on demand.

On some nights I would sit in my chair, the fourth jar on my lap, and start laughing with joy at the success of my restaurant. I would have to force myself to envisage a starving child or departing lover. I knew that there was boundless, ceaseless suffering on this earth, but I found it more and more difficult to identify with it myself, while the prestige of my restaurant grew higher, and with it my bank balance.

I found that the most efficacious manner of forcing tears from my eyes was to think of love; loves lost, love's tragedies and love's hopelessness. And so it was that I began to have trouble with the second jar. Latterly, my attempts at masturbation were rather more difficult, as my erotic thoughts staggered and tumbled into the despair I needed for the fourth jar. Not infrequently, I found it impossible to distinguish between sorrow and love.

After five months, I caught myself ejaculating into my lap, upon which rested the jar meant for tears. I began to find sorrow arousing, and could not cry without getting an erection. Conversely, I could not find a woman attractive without starting to weep.

I worried about my salts, for my supplies were running low. Moreover, the quality of the salt from the first jar was beginning to decline, as I attempted to find solace in alcoholic abandon. I would drink deeply; and laugh, and cry. But my urine suffered. It became thin and pale, copious but worthless. The salt I extracted was tasteless.

The reputation of my restaurant would keep its fortunes buoyant for a while, but I knew that sooner rather than later the decline in the quality of the seasonings would be noted. I sank lower into despair. I could not run the terrible risk of sharing my secret with anyone else. I had only one reliable source of salt – that which filled the third jar. The third jar never ran out. The menu had to reflect this, and there was a preponderance of rich, red, meaty dishes, lavishly enhanced with the salt of my blood, trickled – or sometimes drunkenly spurted, gushed – from my fingers, thumbs, wrists or arms every evening. But I was weakening.

My drinking was becoming uncontrollable, I would involuntarily orgasm during the news, and burst into tears at the most inopportune moments. The constant blood-letting was making me anaemic.

I resolved to return to the formula that had won my eaterie so many plaudits. Determinedly, I researched the most emotionally draining novels, the most haunting poems. I ejaculated again and again into the second jar. I drank pure fruit juice and mineral water and produced once again the golden, viscous urine that filled the first jar. I wept uncontrollably, for three-quarters of an hour, with a pornographic magazine propped in front of me. And I took the sharpest knife and drew one widening red line across my wrist.

The banquet was a success.

Straw

I've got this job now, and there's a great deal of travelling involved. I'm based in London, but most of the work is out in the suburbs. I don't get home really, except at weekends. I was staying with friends to start with, to save money, but the manager said, oh get a grip for fuck's sake. What you doing, kipping on fucking sofas? Fucking state of you. Suit all rumpled to fuck and smelling of dog. Stay in a fucking B&B why don't you. Charge it. It's expenses, ain't it? Fuck sake.

Then he shrugs at me, turns around and goes back into his office. I don't mind sleeping on sofas, but maybe he's right about the smell of pets. It can't be good for business. So I start booking into bed-and-breakfast places, and some of them, well, really I'd rather be on the sofa smelling of dog. But still, I'm not going to argue.

Then I have a truly horrible day. I'm on my way out to somewhere near Romford and I witness a traffic accident and the man who gets hit, well, you can tell he's dead, straight away. It's a terrible scene. He never stood a chance. I drive on, but my hands are trembling, and I pull over after a while, and sit there until I feel a bit better.

Two days later and I'm north of Bromley, sitting in the car having a sandwich when an elderly woman keels over outside the McDonald's opposite. I get out and cross over the road to help but, to my horror, she's dead. There's nothing I can do. I call 999 and wait for the emergency services. When they arrive they don't seem all that bothered, and they put the old lady in the ambulance. I give the policeman a statement and then he just nods and tells me to be on my way. He says that someone will be in touch.

Of course, it's a coincidence, but the next day there's another fatality when my job takes me down to Epsom. It happens again over in Romford, and again three days later up near Waltham Abbey. I start getting really bothered after another two, and over the weekend I can't sleep properly because I can't help worrying that I'm somehow cursed. I mean, obviously, people die all the time, but still.

On Monday night I'm staying in a B&B up in Hendon. I'm chatting to the landlady, and she tells me, in a confidential whisper, that there's only one other guest there, staying in one of the upstairs rooms, and he's really ill. The landlady is worried sick about him. To be honest, it seems that she's more concerned about him dying in her guesthouse than anything else, but I'm actually prickling with anxiety, thinking, oh no, not again, please.

I go to bed, and when I come down for breakfast in the morning the first thing I do is ask the landlady, so, erm, that chap upstairs, is he, um, OK?

The landlady says that he's fine – well, not fine, as such, but not dead. I'm really relieved, and I say goodbye after I've paid up and head out of the door.

I'm just unlocking my car when I realise I've forgotten my bag, so I pop back to pick it up. I'm in the hallway, just about to leave for the second time when I hear this voice from up the stairs saying, help.

It's the ill guest, and the landlady's nowhere to be seen, so I run up the stairs and knock gently on his door saying, are you OK?

No, he says, so I go in to see what he wants. He says that he's dying, and he wants to hold my hand while he goes. I take his chilly hand and hold it and look despairingly at the door, thinking, this is the last fucking straw.

CHOLER

For Modern Living

Always sunny where we live, in old thatched cottages, extensively refurbished, by the pond. Ducks quacking, birds singing, a shiny low-slung German car crunching on the gravel.

Sunlight always on our backs, always blue skies, never rain. A bounding labrador on Sunday walks, no mental illness.

Always sunny, glowing round our hair like haloes. Stress is so yesterday, disappointment so passé.

Always he = *charm* + *smiles*, she = *tilts head to him*: they laugh. Always active in leisure pursuits and work.

We always cook the latest fashions, we always wear sturdy-but-stylish. Our taste is impeccable, our skins flawless [he = *slightly rugged*, her = *english rose w/ attitude*].

Always sunny where we live, in loft conversions, architect-designed, in an up-and-coming area, mobiles cheeping, emails incoming.

My wife?

Works in outsourcing, you must meet her.

My suit? Thank you.

Really? I was talking to them only last week, haven't you heard?

Cappuccinos, meetings.

Here's my car, my wide car, with the marque, the shine,

the model that tells you my approximate income bracket.

Always sunny.

I am effective – *brutally effective* – in meetings.

Money makes money, money meets money, money greets money, in atriums, lifts and restaurants.

I get shown the wine label.

I know what I'm talking about.

I finish with a coffee and a smile.

Always take the money always run.

Always sunny where we live.

No silences in our conversations

[*modern life where everything is possible*].

None of the Above

Like everyone else, I fell into love to the soundtrack of famine and war. During this episode I failed to think much about it. I devoted my attention to the eyelashes and the freckles on her face. I thought about sex also. During my period of falling I was stung by a wasp, failed to recognise my face in the mirror, was the subject of laughter, ate little and infrequently, assumed I was unique, had difficulties with reality, crashed in my car, had mosquitoes feast on my forehead, lost my job and had diarrhoea.

Although none of the above were important to me at the time. I remember them only because I had fallen into love. Do you love me? I love you. Do you love me? I love you.

And nothing else mattered and nothing else happened. The famine and the war were like wallpaper.

If we had been murdered in our beds. If we had been forcibly separated. If our families had been killed. If we had lost our minds. If she had been killed. If I had been killed. If we had been beaten raped tortured stabbed shot tied up with barbed wire dragged along the road behind the tanks

None of the above.

None of that has happened to us yet.

Only a Nightmare

What's the idea? This is the idea: you get into your car that you bought this year on some huge mortgage scheme and will have to replace in another year or so after you've killed a few birds mammals and maybe a child or two and drive to the supermarket past all the dead shops that have been put out of business by the supermarket and park on a huge expanse of concrete that has been put on a field or a wood then walk probably further than you would to a corner shop and commandeer a huge trolley and go into the supermarket and fill up the trolley with things you don't want don't need and can't afford then have an argument with whoever you're with because the whole experience is beginning to destroy you and then you queue up behind a line of similarly soul-damaged people then a poor unfortunate kid or pensioner who probably dreams in bleeps reads the barcodes on everything and doesn't want to hear you say anything and is obliged to ask you if you have a loyalty card and if you want cashback (yes please I'll have the fucking lot back and you can keep all this crap in my trolley) then you have to cart it all back to your car and load it up in the boot and get in and get out of the gargantuan car park then drive home through the bleak wasteland occupied only by those too poor to own a car and unload it all again into your dream home and then consume it all and when you've shat it all out you have to fucking go back again.

Daydream

I'm walking along the lane, thinking vaguely that I am off to fetch the future from my unknown destination. Brown-paper grocery sacks flip along the wet tarmac in the breeze, occasionally adhering to the ground where they slowly leak blood, again and again, to the sound of crows calling in a slow frenzy.

Some Nuclear Reactors

The latitude of the Palo Verde nuclear reactor in Arizona is minus eighty-seven point one three one oh five. The longitude is thirty-four point three eight seven five oh. In California, the Diablo Canyon reactor is minus one hundred and twenty point eight five five four five, then thirty-five point two one one four two. In Florida, Turkey Point is minus eighty point three three one six eight by twenty-five point four three six oh four.

My own location is not so precise. I'm sitting in a chair and I'm staring at the wall.

A Green Park for Business

Men in pink fluorescent coats are burying the dead by the side of the road. They are yawning. There is a solitary figure on the overpass, watching the traffic flow east. Three motionless horses are standing by some wet straw in the rain in a redundant field next to the business park which is all made of green glass held miraculously vertical in the brown mud.

That part is in development.

Next door is what I'd call a showcase. The immense green-glass palaces are spaced perfectly amongst each other, and reflected cumuli flick gently across their surfaces. I like the trees; they are perfect, like the ones in architects' 3D renderings. They have been planted in lines, wide avenues of hopeful saplings bordering new black tarmac car parks, freshly delineated into car-shaped boxes.

There aren't many people at work in these new premises, because it's Sunday. But the cars that belong to people who are either very keen or contractually obliged are parked very well, and at a certain distance from each other. The distance reminds me of the distance between men at a public urinal where there's room for them to be choosy.

I like it that these people are awake and working on a Sunday. It gives me a warm feeling. I'm envious of them. I imagine them in their cars going home along the A roads, or the motorway, and their cars will be warm with the radio playing, and they'll be thinking about something. And they'll turn into the estate of new houses and their house will be in there and they'll know which one it is and they'll drive up and park and get out and lock the car and unlock the front door and everything will be all right.

I like it.

After the green park for business is a big housing estate that looks very new. The gardens have grass and white plastic garden furniture. Some have swings, but I don't see any children. It's quite hard to see much, because there is a high defensive rampart, ten or fifteen feet tall, running the length of the estate next to the motorway. On top of the rampart is a wooden fence to keep the noise of the traffic away.

After I stopped looking.

Except

A lot of the houses out here are bright red, straight out of the paint tube. The fences around their gardens aren't right. But over there, to the east, everything is realistic and local and as it should be, except on fire.

Perspective

Life in our city becomes intolerable and we have to get out. It is very difficult.

We escape to the countryside on the slopes outside the town. But none of the people who live in the country want to help us. We are bringing the plague. I look down at our city. Everything looks strange and perspective doesn't work any more.

We climb the hills into the woods and we really don't know what is going to happen to us.

Sweaters

We listen to the radio sometimes and the politicians and the generals all seem to be OK. They can't commit and often they can't comment either but we often have to do both.

When this is over we will watch the news. Then the politicians will be more precise. They will have novel ways of arranging events. Everything will be OK, and that will be official. It would be hard, otherwise, to tell what had happened.

Murder

Someone standing close to me is shot in the neck. He spins round suddenly very slowly and I can see the hole in his neck where his Adam's apple should be. It is edited like a scene from a film. The crowd scatters and meshes and the man falls. Bad thoughts crowd my head. But the worst thing is that I want to get away as quickly as I can and I can't remember where I have left my coat.

East Croydon

First; wet, black rock. Blue plastic flapping fitfully. There must be a wind. Floodlights on tall posts, or maybe security cameras. Huge plastic sacks full of trash. So much trash. Museums of it. Graffiti painted over in a colour approximating bare concrete.

Below are roads, then a roundabout. A big sign says 'courage', in capital letters. Everything has a coating of limp soggy brown dead leaves. The cars look balletic on the wet tarmac.

Torn scraps of blue sky. Black. Dark. Yellow light.

Obsolete brick sheds with blank windows and extinct chimneys, men in high-visibility vests, housing estates, blackened hedges, lumped fields, sagging parkland, empty barns, ragged fallow, serried conifers, saturated mud, burst banks.

Trees standing staring.

Then; acres of wet, empty rails. Another sign says 'the snooty fox', in italics. Pylons. Pyramids of gravel. Industrial units, Portaloos. Mud. Rubble.

Self-storage. I'd like to store my self. Not needed at present. Will call back later.

An empty football pitch. Studded boots sliding through mud, dog shit. Kwik Fit. Waitrose. Industrial estate. Mobile homes immobile. And a Portakabin remote in a field of trash. A distant mental hospital. Stockbroker homes.

A huge wet field. One man standing in it. Arms raised wide to the sky. The sun finally comes out. We will shortly be arriving in East Croydon.

Inflatable Black-Rubber Stately Home

I remember with an occluded clarity our inflatable black-rubber stately home.

Back in those days we would wander the corridors in a kind of suspended conversation, words drifting like sunlit dust between us as we stepped forward, never knowing. Our feet would crunch the decades of dead insects that had ended against the grimed glass. The sunlight was millimetres away, but unknowable. You looked blankly from the high window and there was not much to see that I could see but probably many decodings for you. The black rubber radiated a claustrophobic warmth but I was cold to my bones and I wished I had a thicker sweater to keep away the shivers. Out behind the window some birds moved through the grey air writing words.

Behind us our past was filled with people and events, talk and activity, engagement and civility. It dragged us upstairs like a ghost. The floors bounced with a forgotten alacrity and there was a joy written there on the walls but all it said to me was *get out, get out*. I couldn't remember the way out, or even if I knew the way in. I was carrying the jars of our dried shared life in a crappy old supermarket bag digging into my wrists and it hurt. I wanted at least a bus home but I was at home in our black-rubber stately home. There was no bus and no home.

In the fuggy behind of my memory our past was flexible and allowable; there was a way to make an impression. Today when I try to make an impression I hurt my head against the wall.

Yesterday I asked if we could take our inflatable black-rubber stately home out again; blow it up, and pretend that nothing had happened. But you said no: our tent would do. I cried my tears into another plastic bag and dropped it, unseen, into a bin.

Midsummer's Day in a Graveyard

Easyjets crawled across the sky, into the west wind. I read: *in loving memory of.* And: *what will survive of us is love, love is eternal, here rests for a time.*

Perhaps the dead lie happily in the well-tended plots, or perhaps they prefer the forgotten, overgrown corners. Perhaps they prefer their names obliterated by time and the weather. Perhaps not.

There was only the sound of the strong west wind in that place, and I wasn't there for very long before I thought that I should leave.

Camera

I took some photographs in a dream. I took so many that I filled a 36-exposure roll of film. I took them to the developer's. They could develop them in 24 hours, 48 hours or 3 days. I was quite excited about the photographs, so I decided to go for the 24-hour service.

When I got the photographs back I was disappointed, because they were all blank, just white rectangles. I thought that perhaps, if I stared at them for long enough, I might find myself back in the dream. I tried this for a while, sitting on a wet bench on a drizzly day in Regent's Park. It didn't work. A mother walked past with her child, who said, 'The sky's not grey.'

But it was.

Camera

[illegible]

Attraction

I pushed through the crowd towards the main attraction. In a big glass tank was a naked man, standing there gazing ahead, not looking at us or anything at all. In the tank with him were millions upon millions of maggots, slowly chewing away at his flesh. As the writhing maggots gorged on the oblivious man, they visibly swelled and grew, and their sloughed skins were drawn along a glass chute by some kind of suction device into another glass tank where they rolled wispily together in their millions, glowing in the Californian sunset.

This was his act; standing in his glass cell, alive and fully conscious, he was stoically bearing his complete consumption by the squirming larvae that surrounded him. By sunset there would be nothing but a sinewy skeletal armature in the tank. And the crowds would leave, holding hands, moving easily into the dusk.

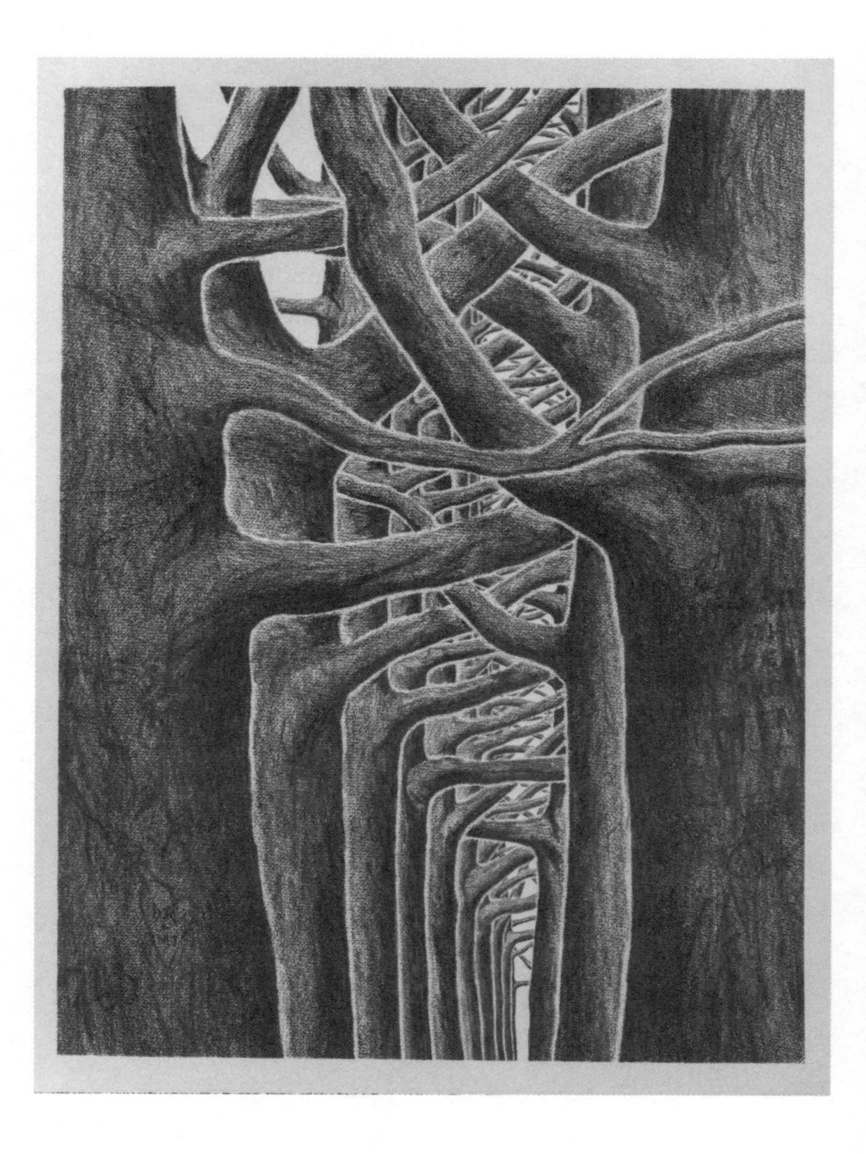

MELANCHOLY

Very Cold

Everything was normal and as it should be until one day I woke up and there was something wrong. I didn't know what it was, but it was a kind of persistent thing that I couldn't quite ignore. Something was cold and it was inside, not outside. It was like a place where someone had poked me with an icicle. A splinter of winter. The days passed like they do and I just got colder. The cold spread until I was like a sculpture of ice. I didn't sneeze any more, and I couldn't cry and if I tried to come it was like a tendril of porcelain. I was a solid man. You could throw rocks at me and it didn't hurt at all. I just splintered a little.

Perhaps fortunately, no one noticed and everything carried on being normal and as it should be, all around me. But I was frozen.

Telescope

The gap between you and me. The gap between you and me. In art class, the teacher would say to look at the spaces between objects. That was how you could see what the objects really looked like. Well. Well, I was fairly certain of your shape. I'd looked at it quite a lot. It was the shape of billowing wheat or sad violin music or a quiet discussion in the coat room at a party, or something. I wasn't so clear on my own. I had looked at it, in mirrors, or in confused reflections from shop windows, and to me it looked unremarkable. Just the shape of some man or other. Could've been anyone, really. When I tried to remember my shape it was the silhouette of a murderer, a torturer, a rapist, or some kind of fiend. There was no end to how bad my shape could be, when I tried to think about it. Our shapes, together? The gap between them was bigger every day. I couldn't see what we really looked like. The only thing I could think of was the sad violin music and the rapist; very far away, never any nearer.

Quiet Beckoning

It is an old house that had once known grandeur but now has faded, moth-eaten curtains, cobwebbed windows whose sills are graveyards of desiccated insects, rising damp, mildewed furniture, dry rot, woodworm, subsidence, peeling wallpaper, rotten carpets, treacherous staircases, choking attics, dead smells, wasp nests, leaking ceilings, creaking doors, collapsed chimneys, grimy sinks, sagging floorboards, rat-shit-scattered corridors, cracked walls, crumbling plasterwork, dry toilet bowls, decades-old newspapers coated with decades-old dust on leaning tables, prone chairs, silent telephones, and vacant, forgotten ghosts who have nowhere else to go.

Though on the ground floor, in the west wing, is one single room where there is a small stove that burns gently through the day and the night. There is a comfortable chair here, threadbare on the arms. There is a narrow bed and a table that is clean. The floor is swept and the window, though small, is open on sunny days.

And if you want to come and see me, I will make you a cup of tea and try to remember.

Romance

I was just staring out of the window, trying to see past my reflection on the rain-streaked black glass of the night-train window. Then I heard a woman saying to a man, 'I thought you only drank one bottle of port and some champagne. Well, more fool me.'

She sounded quite angry, but I didn't know the whole story and for all I knew she could have been completely justified in being angry. There was a kind of mumbling, then she said, 'That's all very well. All very . . . clever.'

I wondered what he had said that was clever. There was a bit more mumbling, and the next time the woman spoke she said, 'I don't want to go there. Simple as that.' Straight away the man hissed at her, 'Simple as what? What exactly?'

I more or less glued my face to the window.

'I mean, you haven't slept with me in weeks. Months,' he hissed again. 'Well,' she said, 'you don't want me to.' The man hissed again, 'It's not surprising. Your tone. It says it all.'

We were the only people in the carriage, hurtling through the lightless wastes of England. Your tone. It says it all.

Island of Doctor Moreau

I married during a sweaty fever of happiness and had been considering distaste for some years when it started. My face and chest began to feel too warm, as if I had run too far. On the morning following our third anniversary I awoke blearily, and padded to the bathroom where I found my mirrored self an impressionist caricature of what I expected. My skin had become my enemy; my self incarcerated within a prison that displayed my unhappiness publicly. I pulled at my features, pressed hard on my cheeks to bring a brief semblance of my previous normality to my face, but the details were all gone. I had to blur my eyes to see my past.

I left our house, and moved like a ghost through the streets, unhappily aware of the sharp three-dimensionality of my surroundings, the microscopic actuality of other people. I took short breaths, the air entering shallowly through my misty nostrils. It was like inhaling through cloth. I needed solitude, and walked quickly to the edge of the town. I passed along deserted roads, scuffing dust, keeping by the high walls in the shadows where I belonged.

It got late, and I worried that the dusk would assimilate me, that I would disperse like blood in the ocean. Reluctantly I returned home. My wife greeted me, and asked after my day. She talked for a while, but I didn't really hear what she said. I sat, morosely prodding at my face, unwilling to look at her eyes. I knew she would be squinting, making small head movements in an effort to force me into focus.

We divorced quite soon after. For a long time I thought that I understood why, but when I asked her one afternoon when we met in a café, she said I had got it wrong. It wasn't that, she said. It wasn't that at all.

Space

During the war I visit some relations in the country. The privations of living for years in a battle zone have hit them hard, and although the war is nearly over they remain locked into the habits of the frightened.

After a frugal meal of potato soup, I am invited to look round the smallholding that surrounds their scarred house. Oddly, in each paddock is a smaller fenced area, sometimes one, sometimes five or six. Puzzled, I ask why they are there.

The reason is simple: each small fenced area represents an animal that has long been eaten. The fences are there to remind my relatives of the livestock they once had. I peer closer, and on each there is a small label – goat, horse, cow. Numbly shaking my head, I walk back to the house.

We speak in hushed tones, discussing the war and the friends we have lost. As dusk falls, a single candle is lit.

The world outside is almost silent, and I have an eerie feeling that we are drifting alone, surrounded by susurrating space.

Faded Notice

Nothing much grew around the village any more, except yellow nettles, giant hogweed and twitch grass. Both of the shops had been closed for ages, with net curtains hung in the display windows, barely concealing the dusty emptiness of the redundant shelves, the avalanche of unopened junk mail below the letter boxes, and the ghosts which left no footsteps on the dirty linoleum floors.

Faded typescript taped to the inside of the door of one shop explained the falling-off of trade, the lowered profit margins, the forlorn blame laid at the automatic doors of the out-of-town supermarket thirteen miles away. I read this notice many times, as if one day it would explain more. There was no such explanation on the door of our house, though perhaps there should have been.

Things had been going awry between us for some time. We had difficulty in understanding one another somehow; as if we spoke different languages and our interpreter had more lucrative work elsewhere. We moved around each other in something approximating silence, in a wan ballet that owed more to exclusion zones than elegance or grace.

Often it seemed as if we were the only inhabitants of the village. On my aimless perambulations I would see no one at all. No dogs, no cats. I saw only birds; crows circling high overhead in the white sky, calling out in the air, laughing, or perhaps crying. Their nests were knotted cancers high in the tallest trees. I watched them as they wrote indecipherable messages against the clouds. Not for me. No messages. I went home, and our front door was heavy as lead.

Lachrymose

My life was dust in a sunlit stairwell; tiny fragments of things that were no longer there, floating aimlessly, sinking slowly. I shared my room with a fly that moved erratically round the light bulb. I copied its movements into a notepad, hoping that they would spell out letters, words, sentences. And that there might be some meaning there.

– on

– and on

– at

– last

Nothing, I thought. The fly lived in my room all summer and never said anything useful. Just round and round the light bulb. Every day. It never seemed to rest, or eat. Maybe it slept when I slept. I didn't know much about that. It doesn't do to think too hard about sleep. Or love, or hunger. Some things get easier with thought, like mathematics. But other things are best left alone. Just going round and round.

I wanted to be like a piece of music played on a piano in a circular room at the top of a tower. When I looked out of the window I wanted to see a rolling pine forest stretching to the horizon. The truth was that my music sounded like traffic and my view was of a wall five metres distant.

★

TEAR WINE

4½ litres (8 pints) tears
1 kg (2¼ lb) white sugar
Juice of 2 lemons
General-purpose yeast

Boil the tears as soon as possible after crying as they can very easily sour. Add the sugar to the boiling tears. Add the lemon juice. Start the yeast in a glass. Leave the tear mixture to cool to blood heat, then add the started yeast. Leave to ferment in a darkened room for three days then strain off into a 4.5 litre (1 gallon) jar and seal with an airlock. Bottle, cork and store when fermentation ceases. This wine may be drunk after a month but it is even better after six months.

– on
– and on
– at
– last

Designer-Outlet Village

I am too late, I am too old, I am late. Perhaps I am apprehensive and weary. We drink coffee from paper cups while we sit in a polystyrene medieval castle. There aren't many people.

The Burger King has a thatched roof and I briefly wonder about the employment prospects for thatchers in this wet, cold and foggy part of the country. I once wanted to be a thatcher, but today I am glad I am a nothing. Whatever. There is a glass roof arching over everything here anyway. And I wouldn't want to thatch a Burger King in a polystyrene castle.

Motorway on such a grey day with fog and the town we drove through was dead and then a slip road and huge signs loom out of the fog saying 'designer-outlet village'. We park in the car park with the other cars.

After walking to the designer-outlet village there is music outside in the fog but it isn't very good music and even without fog it wouldn't be very good. Inside there are a lot of clothes to buy but I don't buy any because they aren't very good. There are a few people from the dead town here and they aren't buying any of the clothes either.

Everyone is very subdued.

This is quite nice, she says to me, holding something with sleeves up for me to look at but I can't find any words.

Perhaps I am apprehensive and weary.

We drink coffee from paper cups while we sit in a polystyrene medieval castle.

Rural Idyll

She said that the couple who own the shop are nosey and given to gossip. If I went to the shop there would be talk in the village, she said. There had been a power cut and I thought it would be a good idea to get some candles in case it happened again.

The shop was shut and it was cold so I didn't hang around. I walked around in the empty village and there wasn't much to see. Some of the houses showed evidence of having once been shops also; there was a plinth and a cross that seemed to suggest a former market place. Sometimes a car went past. But mostly there was just me and my thoughts and a grey sky overhead that may have indicated rain. The rain didn't come which was sort of good and sort of bad.

By the time I got back to the shop it had opened so I went in and I was the only person in it except for the couple who owned it and they just looked at me silently in the kind of way you can feel even when your back is turned.

I got the candles and it was maybe quite exciting to hear the talk in the village after I'd gone but I doubt it.

Beautiful Story About

There's just the muffled crunchy sound of teeth grinding and scraping of boots on tarmac or something and a noise far away that maybe is someone crying or a cat and everything moves a bit in the wind.

There's a tape on of people talking about probably nothing important at a restaurant and a marching sound that's a bit like a lot of soldiers and a bit like a wheel rubbing against metal but it might not be a tape it's hard to tell. And everyone's run out of jokes because no one's laughing at anything although they probably would if they had a sense of humour.

Probably nothing important. Just a noise in the dark when you're half asleep something behind the curtains don't look it's nothing don't look honestly it's nothing.

Maybe it's the town you live in making these noises or maybe it's you. Just a million mobiles and modems squawking and spluttering and hissing like piss on a fire like a million gallons of piss on an inferno just think of that eh?

Just think of that. Vertebrae being sawn apart sounds like this.

And when I opened the curtains they were taking the set away and packing up for the day, the cameras and lights turned off. The darkness, the grey skies, the blind whirring of machinery.

I'd like to write a beautiful story about love:

Snuff

We loved each other so much that sometimes it hurt, even when we were close. I wanted to be her and she wanted to be me. Sex never felt complete, and afterwards we talked carelessly about easy subjects to avoid discussing the ache that bruised us both. So one day, in the kitchen, she cut me and I cut her; gently, slowly, too easily. It was the knife we used for onions and our tears were painful but expectant. We dripped the blood into coffee mugs, then bandaged up and went to bed. We fucked and there were stars but we saw different constellations.

The next day the blood was dry and rusty in the mugs. We scraped it diligently onto sheets of paper. We looked at each other silently and lowered our heads to snort each other's dust. Afterwards we both carried a pouch of powdered blood, and when we were low and apart we would retire to a rest room and sniff, sniff, sniff.

Oh my darling, we went on and on. Our blood was there always, red and viscous, burnt ochre and blowaway. My blood in your nasal membranes, filtering into your capillaries, finding its inexorable way to your heart. Your blood. My nose. My heart. We belonged to each other and we had made our love tangible, real; something that could be weighed and consumed, taken and enjoyed.

It wasn't a surprise when we used the scalpel to shave

flesh from each other's upper arms. We dried the flesh, though it was difficult to desiccate it completely. We used the airing cupboard. The powdered flesh was better; cocaine to blood's speed.

Did it end badly? Did we go too far? Was our love replaced or deleted by want or need? In losing ourselves in each other did we lose the essence in ourselves that the other loved? Did time simply bore us with its slow wearing down?

I have no answers to any of those questions. But now, sitting here in the kitchen, I admit I am scared of the knife, that I can't dig deeply enough to draw blood, that I will have nothing in the morning but red, raised scratches on my arm. I don't want her to cut me.

Did we kill each other, or are we living happily; but only as happily as you are?